The Creators

The Creators

Book 3: Brink of Life Trilogy

Rick Moskovitz

Illustration and design by Mary Verrandeaux

FLUKE TALE PRODUCTIONS

Table of Contents

The most beautiful and deepest experience a man can have is the sense of the mysterious.

My Credo

Albert Einstein, 1932

Where words fail, music speaks

What the Moon Saw

Hans Christian Anderson, 1840

Prologue

LARA CLUNG tightly to her daughter Macklyn as the ground rumbled and rolled beneath her feet. She'd come so far to save her. How could she lose her now? But the man before her and his dreadful glowing machine held all their lives in his powerful hands.

Once she'd revered him, but that was another life, another time. He'd envisioned a utopia no longer ruled by death and built this machine to bestow eternal youth and boundless knowledge and wisdom upon a grateful population.

But now the machine had evolved into a device of astonishing power that could extinguish all life in the blink of an eye and unravel the fabric of the universe. This man had the power either to stop it or to make it happen. Which would he choose?

Lara looked beside her. Natasha Takana balanced like a surfer as the ground roiled with waves of increasing amplitude. Natasha's face was composed, but her eyes betrayed her comprehension of what she saw. The conductor was moving the symphony to its finale. When the last notes were played, there would be nowhere left to go.

Lara looked back at the man. He turned to face her, his blue eyes sparkling with resolve.

"Leave now!" he commanded. "This isn't your fate."

The door to the room swung open. Still gripping Macklyn in her arms, Lara and Natasha fled, trying to outrun the swelling ground and crumbling pavement behind them. This world was doomed. Would they find the portal, if it still existed, to their own world in time to save them?

1

"WHAT IS THE KEY?" thought Natasha Takana as the sequence of molecular base pairs twisted slowly across her field of vision. She'd spent every Sunday morning for as long as she could remember sitting with her parents in the Church of the Double Helix, immersed in the ethereal music emanated from the Coded Word. She'd listened week after week to the liturgy of the church that had been translated from sequences of DNA that didn't code for known biological activity but had been found with the help of advanced artificial intelligence to contain messages from beings in a parallel universe about the creation of humanity.

Almost a decade before Natasha's birth, the discovery of the hidden code within our chromosomes turned science on its head with the possibility that humankind had been created after all by a supernatural intelligence. While there remained some question whether this intelligence had written our entire genetic sequence or just those parts that told its story, the likelihood that a distant hand had a part in crafting our existence led to a new wave of religion that blended seamlessly with science.

Only a small fraction of the code, however, had been deciphered, painting the creation story with a broad brush. It described the origin of the universe in the Big Bang and described the multiverse that had already come into the scientific lexicon decades before. What was new was that a dying civilization in a parallel world, facing annihilation, had reached across the boundary between worlds to preserve its legacy.

What, Natasha wondered, were the events that had driven them nearly to extinction? And had they survived or was their message all that remained, like the light from a distant, already dead star? She longed to discover the details of their history and to learn whatever they could teach us to enable our species' survival.

At 15, Natasha had grown into a formidable young woman. Even in the absence of a MELD chip, her breadth of knowledge, reasoning abilities, and intuition were without peer. She'd mastered the most advanced levels of mathematics and was an acknowledged expert at breaking codes. She'd made it her mission to decipher the remaining details of the Coded Word, but so far the solution had eluded her, just as it had long stumped the most advanced machine intelligence. There had to be a key, but she had no idea what it might look like.

The AI's had discovered the duality of the code. While at least part of the code bore the story of its creators, the code's pattern within the matrix of the repeating structure of the double helix could also be expressed as music that bore the unique signature of its creators. It had been the singular quality of that music that had drawn Natasha's mother into the Church fourteen years ago and had kept Natasha spellbound week after week for so many years.

Now as she watched the helix rotate and examined the repeating molecular patterns of the nucleotide pairs dancing before her, she struggled to find a hidden pattern in those segments of the chromosomes that remained obscure.

"So much of our genetic endowment is shared and defines us as a species," she thought, "and so little of it makes us unique and defines who we are."

Natasha was deeply aware of one particular aspect of her own genetic singularity, the half of her genes that came from her father and had been modified to arrest the aging process. How this would manifest as she grew into adulthood was yet to be seen. She was aware, however, of her remarkable capacity to heal from injury as well as impressive immunity from infectious disease.

3

The helix turned, the molecules danced, and the music played softly in her head.

"The key," she thought. "What is the key?" With all of her musical savvy, she could not identify the key in which this music had been written.

Not of this world," she thought. "Of course, not of this world."

What if the rest of the story was embedded in the musical patterns and not in the code? How could she enable the music to speak to her? Music, she knew, is so much more intricate than language. While language is mostly interpreted in the logical left side of the brain, music speaks to an interplay of many parts of the brain, including the intuitive right side and the limbic system that mediates emotion and primitive instinct. The ability of music to arouse emotion still distinguished human beings from even the most intelligent AIs.

"This isn't a puzzle to be solved," thought Natasha. "It's a wonder to be experienced. The only way to understand it is to immerse myself in it."

Natasha prepared a quiet room, completely empty except for a single cushion in the center on which she sat. She let the music fill the room, closed her eyes, and listened to the melody while she felt the vibrations envelop her. She focused on her breath as she allowed air to fill her lungs, turn, and flow back out again. She sat and breathed as the minutes turned to hours and the hours to days until her body seemed to dissolve, time slowed almost to a halt, and her consciousness floated on the current of the music.

When the concepts first took form from the music, they came not as language, but as pure knowledge, felt more than thought, integral with her very being.

I am eternal. I am newly born. I carry the burden of the ages. I am pristine. I am obscure. I am transparent. I am alone. I am one with the universe. I am an ending and a beginning. Know me and you will know my origins. Understand me and you will know your destiny.

The world I will show you exists only in memory. Where I dwell has no boundaries, no matter, no place in any sense that you would comprehend. I long to be grounded, to touch, to perceive the limits of a tangible self, pressing up against substance that is not me. I long to be in a physical world that I have never known, but is the foundation of my being and the inspiration for your existence. You are the embodiment of my dreams. Together we can be whole.

A beginning. First contact with a promise of more to come. But was the message embedded wholly within the music or was the music just a vehicle for connecting her consciousness with theirs? Had the history already been fully written, a finished monologue, or could a dialogue unfold, with evolving questions leading to ever more elaborate answers? And would this portal ever open to her again?

2

LENA HOLBROOK scanned the Universal Database for ideas for her next story. Five years had passed since her husband Ray's death. She'd resumed her career as a freelance journalist and had garnered a growing readership after her story about a bizarre mind switching experiment that had upended the lives of a dozen people. The perpetrators, an ultra-secret renegade cell within the North American intelligence network, had been tracked down and caught, but committed mass suicide before they could be taken into custody and questioned. The technology behind the switching had self-destructed before it could be analyzed. The victims of the scheme had remained trapped in one another's lives.

For her last story, Lena had embedded herself within the Tribe of 23, a human supremacy hate group dedicated to keeping sentient AI's a subservient underclass without any of the rights and powers of carbon-based humans. Her exposé had been explosive, sparking a widespread backlash against the group. A SPUD had even been nominated to run for Congress in its aftermath.

An obscure item in the social science feed piqued her interest, partly because of its locale, the Willamette Valley in Oregon, which she recognized as the place where Marcus Takana, the Minister of Discovery, had been raised. Agriculture in the Valley had been wiped out decades ago by the scourge of HibernaTurf, her husband's misguided invention, and Marcus' family had been ruined.

But now the land was being cultivated again by a mysterious group that had the earmarks of a cult. They were devoted to natural farming methods that harked back to the methods of the Amish of previous centuries, shunning the automation that underpinned the efficiencies of most modern food producers. Nobody knew where they came from. Their secretiveness had spawned rumors of occult rituals and members with singular abilities. Getting to the bottom of this mystery was just the kind of challenge on which Lena thrived.

When Lena arrived at the destination specified on the UDB, she found a community fortified within a stockade, surrounded by arid land for as far as the eye could see punctuated by a scattering of windmills. As her vehicle rolled up to the massive gate, she noticed sharpshooters atop the barricades, reminiscent of forts in the Old West. This wasn't what she'd anticipated. She hesitated, wondering what danger might lurk beyond the walls. But Lena was accustomed to risk. She'd escaped her brush with the Tribe of 23 after several close calls that nearly cost her her life. She stepped out of the car and looked up at the defenders.

"Who goes there?" shouted the rifleman nearest the top of the gates.

"My name is Lena," she responded. "I'm a journalist."

"You're not welcome here," shouted the man. "We don't like strangers prowling around." He waved her off with his weapon.

"I've come a very long way," persisted Lena. "Could I have just an hour to explain why I'm here?"

The man looked over his shoulder and appeared to be having a conversation with someone within the stockade. When he turned back, the gates began to creak and slowly parted. From the ponderous way they moved, it looked like they hadn't been opened in ages.

"You have an hour," the man said. "Someone will meet you inside."

As she crossed the threshold, Lena felt as though she were crossing into a magical kingdom. The dusty grayness of the land gave way to a lush green landscape as if a black-and-white film had suddenly been painted in technicolor. Just ahead was a cluster of single story buildings that appeared to be shops. Fields of green extended on both sides to the distant walls of the compound, which bustled with activity. And just in front of her car stood a woman, feet spread and hands resolutely on hips, staring at her with an intensity that threatened to burn a hole right through the middle of Lena's face. Her eyes and mouth were framed in bronzed, wrinkled skin. She had to be at least seventy, but she evoked the toughness of a lioness protecting her brood.

Lena stepped out of her car and approached the woman, whose hand was now extended. Lena reached out her own hand to grasp the stranger's.

"I'm Ellie," said the woman with a grin. "You're standin' in my home, Darlin'. State your business."

"No nonsense here," thought Lena. But she couldn't help but like this tough old bird. How would she breach this first line of defense to buy more time?

"I stumbled upon your community on the UDB and found your back to nature culture intriguing," said Lena. "In this overly technological world, I thought you might be a beacon for others to return to fundamental values. I'd like to tell your story."

Ellie looked her up and down, frowned, and spat on the ground. Lena wasn't sure whether the spitting was meant for emphasis or was tobacco juice from the subtle bulge in Ellie's cheek.

"You haven't a clue about our story," said Ellie. "There's no way you could do it justice. And in case you haven't noticed, we don't want to be found. The rest of the world has nothing to offer us but trouble."

8

"If I found you, others can, too. There are some strange rumors on the UDB. It's only a matter of time before someone else gets curious and shows up on your doorstep. You're probably a lot safer with me. If I knew why you were in hiding, perhaps I could help you control your narrative to the outside world."

Ellie shrugged. Her posture loosened a bit and the folds in her face softened. She seemed to accept that Lena meant her and her people no harm. She wasn't going to punish her for the unlucky accident of showing up.

"It can't hurt to talk," said Lena. "If you still want me to leave after we talk, I'll respect your wishes."

Ellie turned and motioned toward the group of buildings. Lena got back in the car, stopped to pick up Ellie, and they rode into town. The streets were dirt and there were no sidewalks. There was no need for pavement because Lena's car was the only powered vehicle in sight. Horses were tied to hitching posts. A few were harnessed to wagons laden with crops or supplies. With Ellie's guidance she parked in front of what turned out to be a diner.

Once inside, they were joined by a young couple, accompanied by a girl of four or five. They were an attractive pair, both appearing in their early twenties, trim and fit. The woman wore jeans, a work shirt, and boots suitable for working on the land, but her flawless porcelain skin appeared never to have seen the sun. Hazel eyes sparkled within the frame of her face and long, brown hair hung in a braid halfway down her back. There was but a flicker of a smile in her greeting, her lips settling instantly to a dead serious straight line.

The man was tall and powerfully built, muscles bulging at the edges of short sleeves on deeply tanned arms. The muscles of his face were rugged, but his tanned skin was as smooth and flawless as the woman's. He could have been a lumberjack, but something about his demeanor had an aura of authority. Lena guessed that he was someone of importance in this community despite his tender age.

The child stood at the table's edge between them. Her hazel eyes resembled the woman's and her mouth was set in the same serious expression, but there the resemblance ended. Her skin was olive and her hair jet black and curly. Lena examined her for any resemblance to the man she presumed to be her father, but found none. The woman whispered in her ear. She nodded and went outside.

Lena was sure she'd never seen any of them before, but something about this woman was oddly familiar. Not so much in her features as in her body posture, the tilt of her head, the way she looked at her. Lena even imagined for a moment a look of recognition in the other woman's eyes.

"Lena," said Ellie. "Meet Lara and Joel. They're like my right and left hands. Don't know what I'd do without them." Then turning to the couple, "Lena here says she's a journalist. She wants to tell our story."

The couple exchanged concerned looks that underscored Lena's appreciation of her role as intruder.

"Let me assure you," began Lena, instinctively addressing Lara first, "that as a journalist, I know how to keep secrets and protect sources. If your intention is to stay under the radar, I won't betray your anonymity. But as I told Ellie, others might find you as I have. So perhaps we can find some common ground that works for us both."

"Why us?" asked Lara. "Of all the places you could have gone, how did you wind up here?"

"Like I told Ellie, I was attracted to your lifestyle, getting back to basics. I thought there might be a lesson here for my readers." Lara's gaze was starting to make her uncomfortable. She shifted her focus to Joel. "But there was also something that intrigued me about this valley. I knew someone who grew up here in a community like yours until HibernaTurf sterilized the land and drove everyone away."

"We appreciate your intentions," said Joel, "but you saw our daughter, Macklyn. She's happy here...secure and innocent, without any idea what dangers lie outside those walls. Our people have suffered tragedy beyond anything you can imagine. All we want is for our children to live in peace."

A blur of motion out the storefront window caught Lena's eye. The child was doing cartwheels on the street with a form and speed befitting an Olympic gymnast. Lara and Joel exchanged a look that told Lena she wasn't supposed to see this. The mysteries of this place were becoming more and more enticing.

"Let me stay a few days," said Lena, "and I won't interfere with your routine. I'll even work for my keep. I'm fit and stronger than I look. I'll take on any job you want me to do. And I promise not to publish anything without your approval."

"And if we approve nothing?" asked Joel.

"Then I'll go home empty-handed. You have my word."

"Forty-eight hours," said Joel, "and then we'll see. We'll look after your car until it's time for you to go. You can get around most of this place on foot."

She would get to stay, but they were taking control of when she would be free to go. That was only fair. They had no reason yet to trust her. She would have to accept her share of the risk.

3

ABRAHAM WALKED along the water's edge and took greedy breaths of fresh salt air. He gazed out toward the horizon and then back across the beach at the cluster of cottages that housed his small band of followers. When he looked again along his path, the sand curved gently before him, the visible arc of the circular outline of the island.

He could walk all the way around it in less than an hour and could run it in twelve minutes. The island was just a mile across and less than a square mile in area, but large enough for Abraham and the ten men and women who accompanied him to thrive, distant from the closest mainland and distant enough from the nearest islands to keep them cloaked in privacy.

As his arms swung, his eyes fell on his brown and sinewy forearms and his rugged hands. He smiled and broke into a run, feeling his powerful legs propelling him forward and his feet striking the surface of the water before embedding themselves in the soft wet sand. Two years on Bethany Island and Abraham still exhilarated in the liberty of his surroundings and the intoxicating vigor of his body.

He picked up the pace. The ground began to blur until he was stopped in his tracks by an agonizing pain that shot through his right foot. As he lay on his side, he watched the sting ray wriggling in the damp sand, trying to free its barb from the bottom of his foot. He reached down, grabbed it by a wing, and tugged sharply, pulling it free. As it caught a receding wave and swam to freedom, the pain in his foot subsided marginally, blood oozing from the wound.

Within less than a minute the bleeding had stopped and the wound was barely visible. Within five minutes, the pain had vanished, and he was up and running even faster than before, grinning ear to ear. This wasn't his first encounter with a ray and wasn't likely to be his last. A few moments of pain was but a bump in the road that only reinforced his sense of vitality. Nothing could stop him.

Feeling so alive was almost enough. He came close sometimes to relinquishing the mission that had brought him to this juncture in his existence. The thought of just being tantalized him, threatening to drive the resolve from his spirit. But fervor would always come roaring back to pluck him from his place in paradise. Lust dies hard and lust for power harder still.

From the deepest recesses of his mind rose memories of other beaches, other times...a warm, spring night in Daytona, making love on the beach in a drunken haze. When he closed his eyes, for a moment the seductive red lips of his lover smiled once more upon him, the image dissolving with the realization that she'd now be ancient and withered if alive at all.

Then he was on the fifth mile of a swim in the icy waters off the California coast, the culmination of his Basic Underwater Demolition training as a Navy Seal, recovering from nausea and vomiting, fighting leg cramps and current and overcome with hunger. His body was young and hard then, too, a prime specimen of manhood testing his limits of strength and endurance. But the level of fitness he now enjoyed would have been unimaginable even then. He smiled as he envisioned making the swim today with ease and leaving his fellow trainees in his wake.

Paradise was also now threatened by another kind of lust that had newly intruded upon his consciousness after decades of dormancy. His vital young body was awash in hormones and longing that, at least for the moment, had no ready outlet. The five men and five women who accompanied him on this journey were the only other human beings within reach. And the combination of the histories

13

they shared together and the biology of the bodies they possessed made the prospect of couplings daunting. Even the first pair to set foot on the island, who'd adopted the names Adam and Eve, failed to consummate a relationship when Adam discovered to his chagrin he was not at all attracted to Eve or, for that matter, to any woman.

Perhaps it was just as well. At least for now, procreation on the island was forbidden. Pregnancies and children would distract from the mission and increase their vulnerability to adversaries. But pregnancy within their kind also carried unknown risks since each of their bodies had undergone the Ambrosia Conversion that completely arrested the aging process. Few such individuals had ever reproduced, and Abraham possessed little information about the results of these unions.

One such offspring was Natasha Takana, daughter of Marcus Takana, who had undergone the Conversion, and his wife Corinne, who had not. Natasha was of particular interest because of her hybrid status and the likelihood that the island's community would eventually need to interbreed with others in order to sustain itself.

Another case would be the child of Connor Campbell and Terra, a former Ganymede operative. Her child was not yet born at the time of Abraham's last fatal encounter with her. Connor had been a mortal at the time of the child's conception, so that child, like Natasha, would be a hybrid. If Connor and Terra were to conceive again, their next offspring would possess immortal genes from both parents since Connor's present body had been converted.

If Abraham could get his hands on any of these children, they would yield crucial information about the breeding of immortals that would both guide the eventual propagation of their community and fill important gaps in the research behind their mission. For now, though, Terra's whereabouts were unknown to him and he was not yet prepared to deal with the wrath of Marcus Takana, who had become fiercely protective of his family after an earlier attempt on their lives.

Abraham bore the responsibility of guiding this ragtag community, symbolic father to a collection of virtual newborns learning to navigate the world in unfamiliar bodies, beset with unaccustomed feelings and desires. And Abraham, too, was newly minted, test driving the body he inhabited and learning all its capabilities and limits. It would be up to him to raise Lazarus to its full potential so that it could complete the mission undertaken years before, for which they'd all given their lives.

4

CORINNE TAKANA sat on the edge of her daughter's bed, holding her hand in both of hers when Natasha finally opened her eyes. Natasha blinked a few times until her mother's face came into focus.

"You had us worried," said Corinne. "You've been sleeping for more than a day and you've kept to yourself for nearly a week." The crow's feet deepened at the corners of her eyes as she smiled. She bent and kissed her on the forehead.

Natasha tried to sit up, but her body felt like lead and all her muscles ached. Immobility and pain were both unusual sensations. She was accustomed to having boundless stamina and to recover from injury or exertion with singular speed. Now she felt as if she'd just finished four or five consecutive triathlons and all the energy had been sucked out of her body. She'd had no idea how physically taxing her spiritual journey was going to be. And if not for the utter exhaustion, she might have thought it had been only a dream.

"When have you last eaten?" asked Corinne.

"I don't know...a few days, perhaps," answered Natasha. "You know how it is with me. I can usually go days without food or sleep." She struggled again to sit up, then settled back on her pillow.

"Wait here," said Corinne. "I'll get you some soup."

When Corinne returned, Natasha had propped herself up with pillows. Corinne fed her spoonfuls of soup like she hadn't done since Natasha was a baby. Natasha relaxed and let herself enjoy being coddled. She savored the flavor of Corinne's tomato vegetable soup, a favorite since childhood, always made from scratch with freshly picked ingredients from the garden. Natasha never took for granted her mother's lovingly prepared meals from natural ingredients raised at home. Few other families enjoyed this indulgence or would even appreciate how special it was.

As Corinne leaned in to spoon the soup into her mouth, Natasha noticed the fine lines at the corners of her mouth and the softer lines around her cheeks. They brought a gentle cast to her expression, but also were an unmistakable sign that she was aging. She'd had a head start of nearly twenty years on Natasha's father Marcus, whose aging had been interrupted in his early twenties and had only recently resumed. And it was a reminder that Natasha was likely to vastly outlive both her beloved parents, who would be vulnerable to diseases to which she would always be immune.

"You can't imagine where I've just been," Natasha said as Corinne set the empty bowl aside. "It was like visiting heaven and talking to God."

She told Corinne about how she'd followed the music and let it take her to a place where she could join with its creators and receive their message. It hadn't felt at all risky, but now she wondered. Would it be safe to visit again? How much could even her extraordinary body endure without risking her life? It felt almost as though she'd been drawn through a black hole.

"My fearless child," said Corinne after hearing her out, "I can guess already how you'll choose. You've never backed away from a challenge. But please be careful. Even you have limits and I couldn't bear to lose you."

Natasha gave herself a week to regain her strength and gird for her next encounter with the creators. Now that she'd crossed the portal once, she hoped that it would yield more easily to another approach. She set the music playing, sat on her cushion in the middle of the room, and focused on her breath.

This time it felt as though the music had come for her, sweeping her up within it and penetrating her spirit. She felt herself rising, then moving in what seemed like every direction at once. She struggled to keep her body from flying into pieces.

When she came to rest, the first thing she noticed was a distant, shimmering turquoise glow from above and realized that she was looking at the source through a liquid medium in which she was thoroughly immersed. She was no longer aware of breathing, but neither was she hungry for air. And as strange at this place seemed, she felt entirely at home.

She swept her arms behind her and glided smoothly forward, then flexed her ankles and floated upward toward the light. The freedom of movement was exhilarating, reminding her of watching people floating weightlessly in space. But unlike tumbling in the vacuum of space, the gentle resistance of the fluid enabled her to navigate effortlessly in any direction or to be still for as long as she chose.

When she extended an arm before her eyes, she saw long, slender fingers with translucent webbing connecting the proximal digits. When she looked at her feet, she saw four long toes on each foot, connected with webbing all the way to their tips, enhancing her propulsion through the liquid.

The liquid...was it water? Certainly something like water. Perhaps heavier...or more viscous. Clear and colored mainly by the light from the distant orb shimmering through the surface. Yes, there was a surface, but whatever was above remained shrouded in mystery.

She sensed a presence by her side, long fingers reaching out to touch hers. Another form slipping through the liquid tugging her gently along by her fingertips, silently fluttering webbed feet, propelling them both ahead. She glanced at her new companion, a shimmering humanoid in violet and aqua, scales covering the backs of its arms and legs, its torso slick and iridescent. She ran her free hand down the front of her own body, which felt silky smooth, then down between her legs, where she felt a single protuberance above a cleft. She looked again at her companion and saw a similar combination of male and female parts. Strange...and yet familiar. Other...and yet self.

Her companion turned to face her. She gazed upon a visage of exquisite beauty, human and not human all at the same time...genderless, symmetrical, unsullied by ears or nose, appendages that would be needless in this watery world. The eyes gazing back were lavender, round, and bottomless, seeming to draw her deeply within. A pair of slits along the neck culled whatever crucial nutrient was this species' version of oxygen. No breathing...no effort.

She was on a guided tour of a new world, perceiving it through the eyes and mind of a native. And the longer her mind joined with this other being, the more she remembered about its world.

The blue-green orb was this world's sun, its redness extinguished as its image plunged toward her from the surface. Its heat and radiation were both greatly attenuated as its energy filtered through the water, which seemed to stay at a constant, imperceptible temperature that must have been identical with the temperature of her body. And of course, they were all naked. The environment was so completely in sync with their bodies that there was nothing from which they needed protection. And modesty had no relevance in such a world, especially when everyone looked more or less alike.

The planet's gravitational force was exquisitely balanced by the buoyancy of its liquid environment, rendering all motion effortless. It felt like paradise. What could possibly have gone amiss in such a perfect world?

She looked again into the eyes of her guide and felt overwhelmed by sorrow beyond comprehension. Their fingers parted and she sensed that this visit was coming to an end. The sun was setting and its light beginning to fade. She felt her chest swell with an influx of air and her attention was back upon her breath. She closed her eyes and followed her breath through a few dozen cycles. When she opened them again, she was home.

How much time had passed during her visit to the other world? Hours or days? Natasha looked at the time. The clock had barely advanced...less than a minute. The passage of time in this world had no relevance in theirs.

She felt tired and hungry, but not as drained or battered as she had after her maiden voyage to the other world. Perhaps she was getting the hang of riding the currents and waves of the music. It was like learning to surf, catching the wave as it crested and maintaining her balance as it curled and rolled toward the shore. Except this was a metaphysical wave rolling across all space and time, breaching the boundaries of our universe and breaking on the shores of another dimension.

At the far reaches of her awareness, a new sensation began to form. It began alongside her hunger as a feeling in her gut...a sense of a void, an emptiness, something missing that was distinct from physical hunger. A tear trickled down her cheek, accompanied by just a hint of the sorrow that she had so profoundly felt toward the end of her journey. Then she recognized it...homesickness, a profound longing to return to the familiar, the comfortable. But she was already home. Wasn't she?

She closed her eyes and drifted back in her mind's eye to the other world. This time it was as a memory, but a memory with all the intricate detail and fidelity of a childhood home and a lifetime of familiarity and attachment. And the memory included details of things that she hadn't seen during the journey.

There were villages, hive-like structures suspended in circular clusters around larger cylindrical structures and attached to the central structure by spikes resembling corals that kept the clusters rotating slowly together. Beings like her floated within the boundaries of these villages. The hives, she realized, were their homes and the cylinders the control centers of the communities, their seats of power, both social and physical.

While all of the beings strongly resembled one another, she could identify some differences that defined generations. There were juveniles, even infants clinging to the backs of some of the adults, the mother-fathers. And there were elderly, defined more by an altered tempo of their movements than by distinctions in physical characteristics. Slower...yet at the same time more graceful and regal than their younger counterparts.

But there were also other life forms teeming beyond the perimeters of the villages, including many varieties of exotic fish as well as larger animals that closely resembled dolphins. She remembered the pinging sound of the sonar with which these larger creatures communicated and realized that in that world she could not only understand their meaning but could communicate back with them.

As she contemplated these memories that weren't hers, she realized that the portal opened in more than one direction. She was no longer alone in her body, but had brought back with her a fragment of the consciousness of the being with whose mind she'd joined on the other side. There was no turning back from her quest. Her symbiotic partner, bound to its own world, would draw her back with it across the breach. The price of knowing the creators would be entwining her consciousness inexorably with theirs.

5

AS LENA SETTLED into the sparsely furnished cabin for the night, rain was beginning to fall. The gentle tapping of raindrops on the roof intensified to the rhythm of a drum roll before exploding in torrents. Lightning crackled in the distance, followed by the long, slow rumble of thunder. The sounds of a storm were like a symphony to Lena. After years of living with Ray in his underground bunker, living close to nature was both exhilarating and restful.

Before turning in, however, there was research to be done. Lena started by putting Joel's image through the facial recognition database. His face was a match for Tobias Batie, who'd disappeared mysteriously around five years ago in Tennessee. He was, in fact, originally the lumberjack that his body type had suggested when Lena first saw him. He'd somehow acquired a small fortune years before his sudden disappearance and had built a construction empire selling prefabricated log homes. The company was run for the next few years by one of its vice presidents, but eventually fell into ruin without Tobias at the helm. He'd never married, left no heirs, and had been presumed dead.

And yet, here he was, living under an alias with a wife and child. Why would he have abandoned a fortune? How did he wind up in the Willamette Valley? Another tantalizing mystery.

Lena prepared to run Lara's image through the database, but sleep overcame her before she could finish. It had been a long day and the sound of the rain lulled her to sleep.

The drumbeat followed her into her dreams, accompanied by the sound of trumpets. She was watching a parade on Bourbon Street in New Orleans. It was Mardi Gras. All around her were figures masked in pure white porcelain, like the color of Lara's skin. As the figures danced and twirled, flaming red hair swirled all around. One of the dancing figures stopped right in front of her and looked straight at her. Through the holes in the mask glowed eyes of emerald green. Lena woke with a start.

"No, couldn't be," she thought as she shook off sleep. She'd seen Terra only twice and briefly. Once when Terra had met with Ray after a bizarre night when he'd seemed like another person altogether. What she'd later learned about Ray's deal with the devil had finally made sense of that night. Terra had been the devil's agent, the person who had plunged them into the insane misadventure that had ended with Ray's death. The second time was when she watched her die, shot through the back of her head.

The resemblance was so remote. Lara's skin color was eerily like Terra's, but nothing else matched. And yet, there was something else familiar. She couldn't put her finger on it. Her subconscious mind was working overtime in her dreams to solve a mystery.

Lena ran Lara's image through the database. There were no matches. The closest match was only 43 percent, just a little better than chance. It was to Petra Kresky, the daughter of Syrian immigrants, who'd been suspected in Boston of murdering her husband and had disappeared five years ago without a trace. Her body had never been found. Lena pulled up a virtual file image of Petra and stared at it.

Black curly hair. Olive skin. Little resemblance to Lara. But the eyes, hazel, were a pretty close match. What struck her most, however, was Petra's uncanny resemblance to the child, to Macklyn, the sprite who could turn somersaults over the finest athletes on the planet.

Here was a puzzle beyond Lena's wildest imagination: a lumberjack from Tennessee and a suspected murderer from Massachusetts, both disappearing without a trace around the same time five years ago and turning up on a farm in Oregon under assumed names within a community that seemed to have secrets of its own. Tobias and Petra, but not exactly Petra.

Lena fell back asleep with the mystery still dancing in her head. When she next opened her eyes, the sun was just peeking over the horizon through the east facing window of her cabin. There was a knock on the door. When she opened it, she found a neat pile of work clothes at the threshold, topped with a heavy pair of leather work boots. They were calling her on her offer to earn her keep.

Lena changed into the clothes, which fit her perfectly and admired herself in the narrow mirror on the back of the door. For the next few days, she would be a ranch hand. The role appealed to her.

She emerged from the cabin to the sound of a ringing bell. She followed the sound to a mess hall, where dozens of people were sitting down to eat. She spotted Ellie and Joel and went to join them.

"This is the 'little breakfast'," said Ellie, pushing a bowl of yogurt across the table. "A light meal and some coffee gives us fuel to start the day. We work in the cool of the morning for a few hours until the heat starts to roll in. Then we'll have a proper breakfast. You won't believe how good it will taste."

Lena spooned some of the yogurt into the small bowl in front of her. She held her cup out to a young man holding a coffee decanter and gratefully accepted her pour.

"What kind of work will I be doing?" Asked Lena between sips. Ellie and Joel exchanged mischievous grins.

"Joel will show you when you're done with your coffee," said Ellie. "Take your time, Darlin'. The job isn't going anywhere."

When she was ready, Joel led her out to one of the paddocks, let her in the gate, and handed her a shovel. He waved his hand in a broad arc across the area within the fence.

"Your job will be to move the piles of manure from the grazing area to the composter over there." He pointed to a cluster of bins in the farthest corner of the paddock.

Lena understood the meaning of the grins. This was either a test of her sincerity, a playful joke, or both.

"Make no mistake," said Joel, addressing the silent question in her eyes. "This is important work. You will be assisting in the circle of life as the animal waste is turned into rich nutrients for the soil that grows our crops. Every member of this community has done this very job at some point in their life here. It's one of the most sacred interactions with the land." Joel's voice and expression were solemn.

Lena dug in and began filling the wheelbarrow she was provided with horse dung, then wheeling it across the paddock and dumping the contents into the first of the bins. The smell was overwhelming at first around the composting bins, but after a while she stopped noticing it. As she slipped into the rhythm of the job, the weight of the shovel seemed to lessen, and the time passed quickly.

When the sun had risen halfway from the horizon to its apex, she noticed Macklyn balancing on the top board of the farm fence that surrounded the pasture. She was walking on it like a tightrope, stretching her arms out wide. As her pace quickened, her arms came down by her sides and she trotted along as if she were on level ground without a care in the world. One of the horses trotted up alongside her, trying to get her attention, then gently nuzzled her.

As gentle as the nudge was, it disturbed the child's footing and she tumbled from her perch, landing on her left arm and leg. Lena dropped her shovel and rushed to the child's side. Macklyn was already getting up by the time she got there. There were abrasions on her knee and a cut just below her elbow. Lena kneeled beside the child, untied the bandana around her neck and applied pressure to the cut to stop the bleeding. When she lifted the cloth from the wound, the bleeding had already stopped. Lena stuffed the bloody cloth into a pocket as Macklyn ran off again to play. In the distance she spotted Lara, who had watched the interaction with concern.

Back in the mess hall, Lara sat down across from Lena. Platters of food were laid on the table. There were freshly baked loaves of bread, butter, and raw honey, omelets loaded with vegetables, more yogurt, and fresh fruit. Lena dug in with gusto. Ellie was right. Everything tasted wonderful after working up an appetite in the field.

"Thanks for looking after Macklyn this morning," said Lara. "Sometimes it's hard to keep up with her."

"She seems absolutely fearless," said Lena. "I held my breath watching her walk along that fence."

"She seldom gets hurt. Usually it's when one of the animals gets playful. They consider her one of their own."

"An extraordinary child," said Lena.

Lara avoided eye contact and didn't respond to the comment.

"Are you married?" asked Lara, changing the subject.

"I'm widowed. My husband died five years ago."

"I'm sorry to hear that." Something in Lara's tone gave Lena the impression that she'd already known the answer.

"Do you have children?" asked Lara.

"My husband didn't want children. Ray was a very anxious man. They would have intruded upon his meticulously curated life." Her own words surprised her. She'd thought she'd long since let go of her resentment. "But I got pregnant shortly before he died. My daughter will be six in just a few months."

The door swung shut across the room, a welcome distraction from further prying into her complicated past.

"There's Joel," said Lena pointing past Lara.

Lara swung her head around to look and her braid followed in slow motion behind her, swinging back part way before coming to rest. Lena's mind flashed back to the figures in her dream with the red hair swaying to and fro. In her mind's eye, she superimposed the motion of Lara's braid and the hair in the dream. They were in sync. But why not? The dream images were just a product of Lena's subconscious, drawn as much from the residue of the day as from memory.

Alone again in her cabin that evening, Lena drew the bloody bandana from her pocket, where it had stayed hidden through the day. The blood had dried, but still contained its genetic fingerprint. Lena scraped a sample from the cloth with a pocket knife and deposited it on the tip of her tongue, exposing it to the digestive enzymes in her mouth. She uploaded its structure via her MELD chip to the UDB and compared it to the worldwide genetic database.

Macklyn's DNA was most closely matched by two fugitives from justice, one of whom had vanished five years ago and the other killed by gunshot around the same time. She matched 47% of her genome to Petra Kresky, the woman suspected of murdering her husband Arlo. She was a 48% match to Connor Campbell, a man also suspected of complicity in the death of Arlo Kresky and who had been shot at the end of a maniacal rampage on a farm in Maryland in which he'd hacked to death a dozen members of his community. According to the data, Macklyn was the daughter of two murderers.

A search of the facial recognition database identified Ellie as Lily Campbell, the matriarch of the Maryland community on which Connor Campbell's massacre had occurred and Connor's mother. One version of the story on the UDB was that Lily had ended the massacre by shooting her own son. No wonder they'd gone to such lengths to fall off the face of the earth. Such unspeakable tragedy. Lena suddenly felt the weight and responsibility of sharing their secret.

Lena tucked away the blood-soaked rag. It may yet hold the key to other mysteries about this remarkable little girl who moved like a nymph and seemed oblivious to the nefarious circumstances of her birth.

She sunk into the water in the claw foot tub in a corner of the cabin and let it wash away the grime and sweat of her labors. She was dog-tired and ached all over. But it was a satisfying fatigue, the product of honest work. She could get used to this life, at least for a while, long enough for her story to emerge, a story she might never get to write.

6

ISHMAEL COILED the hand line of the cast net in his right hand, looped the net over his hand, and took the weighted lead line in the fingers of his left hand. He turned his body in an arc to his right, paused, and flung the net into the surf. When he pulled it in, he held the net by its horn and shook. The silvery pinfish reflected the sun's rays as they flopped about on the beach.

The first times he'd attempted this procedure, he'd failed miserably, retrieving an empty net time after time. But after months on the island, he'd become expert at all aspects of fishing and was one of the most consistent providers of food for his community. This was a far cry from his previous life as a military officer and later as a covert operative. It had appealed to him for a while, but the isolation from the rest of the world was beginning to wear thin.

He gathered the baitfish in a bucket of seawater and prepared to throw the net again. The sky was getting dark and the wind was rising and whipping through the tops of the palm trees. The water turned from turquoise to gray, peaked with white caps as the surf pounded the shore. The bait could wait. It was time to find shelter from the coming storm.

Would the storm blow over in time for him to make his move that night or would he have to wait another day? Every delay increased the odds of Abraham discovering his plan and thwarting his escape. And Abraham's wrath would be awful, perhaps even fatal.

In his prior incarnation, Ishmael had been a devoted soldier of Ganymede and a loyal follower of Abraham, or the Director as he'd then been known. When they'd begun their mission, it had seemed noble, developing life extending and consciousness swapping technologies to undermine the power of ruthless dictators. But as their operation became more and more divorced from the rest of the intelligence community, it morphed into something that itself began to feel like an autocratic grab for power.

When the Director conceived the plan to replace someone at the highest level of our own government, creating a virtual Manchurian Candidate to do his bidding, he'd crossed a line.

Ishmael had been relieved when Terra had returned to stop them and they'd all died self-inflicted deaths by cyanide, but he'd gone along with the Director's plan for them to reassemble as a team in their new bodies. It seemed the safest way to begin navigating the world as a newborn. Once Abraham plotted to recreate Ganymede's technology and resume the mission, Ishmael began looking for a way out.

Their South Pacific island was miles from the nearest civilization. Abraham controlled the only powered boat on the island. There were a few skiffs and half a dozen kayaks. Reaching the mainland in a kayak would be arduous, but Ishmael, like the others, possessed extraordinary strength and endurance. He had no doubt that he could make the journey, but was less certain whether or not he could evade Abraham long enough to reach safety.

Ishmael had been preparing his escape for weeks. He'd acquired a particularly well-equipped body with resources that would come in handy during the various stages of his flight. His host, Dev Renner, had invested the fortune he'd acquired in exchange for his body and parlayed it into even vaster wealth that he'd parceled as cryptocurrency across a series of wallets on the Dark Web. He'd also had the wisdom to invest in a MELD chip that now enabled Ishmael to indulge in information from the outside world, including information and resources on the Dark Web.

Over the past several weeks, Ishmael had located a sizeable portion of Dev Renner's fortune, retrieved it, and deposited it in accounts that he'd access once back in civilization. It would help him stay hidden from Abraham and the rest of the Lazarus community and might eventually enable him to join forces with Terra and to sabotage the mission.

The seas began to calm as dusk approached. Blue sky peeked through clouds that were now white and streaked with pinks and reds. A rainbow rose from the horizon to his left in a partial arc, disappearing in the clouds. The storm was over, and he saw the rainbow as a sign. Tonight was to be the night.

Back in the privacy of his cottage, Ishmael found a sharp paring knife, washed and dried it, and looking in a mirror cut a circle of flesh from his neck just behind his right ear. He popped the small metal sphere from the hole, wiped it clean, and placed it under his pillow, then pressed the skin back in place. Blood oozed for several minutes, then stopped. The disk of skin adhered to its place.

Once darkness had fallen, he scooped the transducer from under his pillow, slipped silently to the back of the island and found the kayak where he'd left it on the beach. He found a piece of driftwood, hollowed out a small round niche with his knife, placed the transducer inside and wrapped it tight with fishing line, then loaded it into the kayak. He pushed the vessel into the water and glided silently away. He'd have a good head start before Abraham would miss him and begin the search. Finding him on the open sea without his transducer would be challenging. Once on land, he hoped to melt into anonymity.

A couple of miles offshore, the westbound current branched into northerly and southerly streams. Ishmael set the piece of driftwood afloat in the southerly stream, then turned the kayak sharply to escape its pull and paddled furiously until he'd entered the swirl toward the northwest.

His decoy would drift in the general direction of Tonga, while he made his way toward Samoa.

As day broke across the water, land appeared in the distance, first as a jagged mountain peak, then as the outline of a beach. With his extraordinary strength and the help of the tradewind currents, he estimated that he'd traveled around 35 miles in his northwest journey from Abraham's island toward Samoa. There were enough small islands in the intervening distance to shelter and hide him along the way. Even if Abraham guessed that he'd chosen Samoa as his destination instead of Tonga, he would be nearly impossible to track among the islands dotting this swath of ocean.

With his last few powerful strokes, Ishmael glided onto the beach and collapsed on the sand. He was bone tired, hungry, and parched with thirst, but from past experience, he knew his body would regenerate within an hour or two. Once enough of his strength had returned to make his way inland and he'd hidden the kayak behind a sand dune and covered it with palm fronds, his first quest was to find fresh water. Given the rainforest on the slopes of the mountain, that didn't take long. He hiked toward the sound of rushing water and emerged through the trees to see a powerful waterfall terminating in a pool of blue and green. He waded into the cool water to his waist and cupped handfuls of crystal-clear water to his mouth with his hands.

Ishmael was never worried about finding food. He'd brought a cast net and fishing line with him on the kayak and was confident that his skills as a fisherman would serve him well. But here he found an abundance of edible vegetation, including ripe breadfruit and bananas on the trees and taro in the ground. With a little time in his folding solar cooker, they would all provide enough nutrition to fuel the next leg of his journey. With the rate at which his body burned energy with exertion, a diet leaning heavily toward carbohydrates was advantageous.

He would take shelter in the forest by the waterfall until the midday heat subsided before undertaking the next leg of his journey. After filling up on his bounteous meal and fresh, cold water, Ishmael slipped into a peaceful slumber, free at last.

7

THE MUSIC NOW PLAYED softly, continually in Natasha's head. It was there in the background when she awoke, stayed with her throughout the day, and even followed her into her dreams. It resided in what felt like a parallel consciousness, flowing simultaneously but separately from her attention to the here and now and allowing her to engage with her life without distraction. But from time to time the cadence rose and swelled, beckoning her across the divide to let it carry her back to her other home.

Crossing over to the other world, she realized, would now be a matter of simply surrendering to the music that was already inside her. She no longer needed to generate it in physical form. And surrender would no longer be a choice, but would depend upon the tug of war with the metaphysical hitchhiker that had accompanied her from its own world. Understanding that she was no longer in control, Natasha let go of her need to know when the balance would shift and she would embark on another expedition of discovery.

The music next took her days later during the twilight state of sleep. It carried her so gently this time that she thought at first that she was dreaming, but she recognized her destination by the absence of her breath. When she opened her eyes, she was immersed in the watery fluid, but this time was peering through a convex window at the vast expanse of water from within a room.

The room was nearly spherical in shape, with several openings spaced over the interior surface. She fluttered her feet and glided through one of the openings to emerge into an identical space. As she moved from opening to opening, all the spaces appeared the same, each with a convex porthole looking out at the surrounding space. Through the portholes, the fluid seemed murkier than before and the orb of the sun fainter when visible at all.

She was inside one of the hives that she'd remembered during the interval between visits. She could see the blurry outlines of some of the other hives radially connected by spikes to the same control center as hers. Strikingly absent, however, was any sign of people in the space around the hives. She could tell that she'd returned to a different time, another chapter in the history of this world, but had no idea how much time had passed between the scene of her first visit and this one.

She heard a pinging in the distance and turned her head to gauge its direction. She followed the sound through the labyrinth from opening to opening until she found herself floating inside a tube toward a bright light at the other end. When she emerged, she was in a cavernous vertical space inhabited by dozens of others, all intently focused upon a column of images at its center. As she moved around the central column and looked over the shoulders of the people, she could see that what appeared inside the column changed with the angle at which it was viewed so that the perspective of each viewer was unique. But unlike a hologram in which only the perspective changes as one moves around it, these images were all of distinctly different objects each occupying the same space.

She watched the long, partially webbed fingers of her companions moving deliberately and rhythmically in the water while watching the space before them. They were each operating upon the object of their unique vision, collaborating on changing something about the entity that fused all the visions together. She was observing the function of an advanced data processor, networking together a community of operators in a synchronous dance of gestures the objective of which they all seemed to understand.

Natasha noticed an empty station around the circumference of the column and took her place in the network. The image before her resembled a flickering flame, orange and green, dancing in place. She felt her fingers moving and realized that she was working to steady the image and rotate it into position as part of what appeared to be an intricate multidimensional jigsaw puzzle. Each member of the team was working to coordinate the other pieces of the puzzle. What were they building?

As the components interlocked, the column began to spin, first slowly, then faster and faster like an enormous corkscrew with waves originating at its point and rising to the top of the column in continuous succession. It was a dynamo, integrating energy from the currents surrounding the hives to provide power to the community. As the turning dynamo gained speed, the fluid immediately around the hives became clearer and was suddenly populated by swarms of fish and a phantasmagorical array of colorful creatures, all vying for a place near the hives.

The most essential function of the generator that had been set into motion was to power the filtration system that kept the fluid within the hives and a perimeter outside the hives clean and compatible with life. In the time span between Natasha's first visit to this world and this one, the population had expanded and technology had advanced, the most salient effect of which was to foul the waters in which they lived and drive them inside the hives permanently, where their environment could be controlled. Additional clean water could be generated to create a space around the hives hospitable to enough sea life to harvest and feed them, at least for a while.

"What could possibly go wrong?" she'd wondered during her first visit to Paradise? Even on this world, the inhabitants would not possess Eden forever and were destined to be banished, confined to the labyrinthine hives they had originally designed only for shelter and rest.

Now she wondered how long they could sustain themselves within this fragile equilibrium. The advance of their technology had served them poorly. Could further advances save them from starvation and extinction?

Natasha opened her eyes. The sun was beginning to rise outside her window. She heard birds greeting the dawn with their carefree song. And she felt her chest rising and falling with the flow of her breath. The music still played softly in her shadow consciousness, but beckoned no more, at least for now.

She remembered the hives and the supercomputer and the murky waters and the generator that powered the filters that sustained life in the other world, life threatened eventually with extinction. Could this have been a dream? Could her mind have concocted this next chapter of the civilization's history from what she'd learned during her first visit to their world?

She dressed, ate a light breakfast, and walked outside. It was a balmy June day, the warmest so far of the season, a perfect day for a swim. When she was eight or nine years old, her parents had argued about whether or not to install a pool behind their house. Her mother thought it would be a waste of precious resources, but the water shortage had ended, at least in the DC area. Her father saw it as an opportunity for Natasha to exercise and condition her body, although thanks to the immortal component of her genetic endowment, she was naturally fit and toned.

She stood by the edge of the pool, still fully dressed, gazing at the dark textured surface beneath the crystal-clear water. In a moment of impulse, she stripped off her clothes and dove into the deep end. She was ordinarily modest and would never have considered a naked swim, even when nobody else was within sight. Sliding through the water she felt wild and free. As she felt the water slip between her legs, she glanced down, half expecting to see the ambiguous genitalia of another species.

Her body looked normal, but something had changed. Behind the music's track was a new sound, a series of hollow pings that varied in pitch, becoming higher as she approached the walls of the pool and lower as she moved toward the middle. Even more curious, the sounds did not seem to be coming through her ears, but rather through her skin, as if pressure was being transformed into sound. Hanging vertically and stationary in the middle of the pool with her eyes closed, she could easily distinguish the long dimension of the pool from the short dimension.

When she emerged from the pool, the pinging stopped. She heard a car approaching the house and ran inside to get dressed, suddenly feeling embarrassed by her nakedness. She wondered whether this newfound ability to echolocate had come after her first journey to the other world or was a mark of her return from another visit, proof that it had not been just a dream.

That evening as she ran on the turf in the Endless Park as had become her habit, like her father's in his youth, around dusk, she was overwhelmed by a virtual avalanche of pings, accompanied by hundreds of needle-like sensations all over her exposed skin. She thought she was surrounded by a swarm of stinging insects, but none were to be seen. Instead, way overhead was a dense flock of tiny birds.

"No...not birds," she thought. "Bats!"

She'd seen the bats on other runs, migrating from their perches tucked beneath the eaves of mansions beside the park to feed on insects on the pond at its center. And she'd heard their high-pitched shrieks as they passed overhead, but with her ears, not her skin, and not as pings that rose in pitch as they approached and fell as they moved away.

Here was her proof. She'd been back to the world of the creators and returned changed yet again with a new ability, echolocation, that she shared with the bats in the air, and presumably with the dolphins and whales in the sea.

8

AS LENA DRIFTED off to sleep, she heard the faint sound of bells in the distance, at first resembling the dinner bell that announced mealtimes in the compound. As they increased in volume, she recognized the cadence as a church bell sounding the hour. Twelve bells. Noon time.

She was crouching behind a sofa on a hotel balcony outside a ballroom. People were running panicked in all directions at once. Her eyes were riveted upon one corner of this drama, a hand to hand struggle by the railing between a giant of a man with thick, wavy blond hair and a wiry woman with flowing red hair. Despite the uneven match, the woman prevailed, flipping the giant over the railing by his feet. She heard his body crash upon the ground below.

Out of the corner of her eye, she saw Ray on the balcony, yelling a warning at the woman, but it was too late. A hole opened in the back of her head and blood gushed out before her lifeless body crumpled to the floor.

Suddenly, the balcony was empty except for Lena and the redhead's body, lying on its face. She walked up to the lifeless form, knelt beside it, and rolled it over. Lara's face stared back through lifeless, hazel eyes. She heard a child weeping behind her and turned to see Macklyn in a corner of the balcony, watching them both.

A knock on the door. When she opened her eyes, the sun was already partway up the sky and the breakfast bell was ringing. She sprung from the bed, hastily donned the fresh set of work clothes that had been laid out by her door, and trotted to the mess hall. The images from her dream intruded into consciousness along with the sound of the church bells.

41

"Why does she still haunt me?" thought Lena. "What can this all mean?"

When she stepped inside the mess hall, her eyes went first to Lara, sitting across the room. She heard Ray's voice shouting "Terra" in her head and resisted the impulse to shout it herself. Then Macklyn ran up beside her and squeezed her hand. She'd made a friend over the incident in the corral. Macklyn looked up and smiled at her.

Lena's eyes went straight to Macklyn's elbow, where there was no longer any sign of the gash that had opened when she'd hit the ground the day before. Good as new. How could this be?

She'd seen such rapid healing only once before. Marcus and Corinne Takana's daughter Natasha possessed this same remarkable power. In Natasha's case she knew the reason. Natasha's father, Marcus, had undergone the Ambrosia Conversion before she was conceived that was designed to arrest the aging process and conferred remarkable physical properties, including accelerated healing. The half of Natasha's genome that came from Marcus was responsible for her extraordinary physical prowess. Could Macklyn be another such child? And if so, which of her parents was the donor of the magic strands of DNA?

"Did you sleep well?" asked Lara.

"Like a rock. My body was exhausted from yesterday's work."

"You did well," said Lara. "You did the work of a woman half your age."

"Will I have the same job this morning?"

"No. This morning you'll work with me. We have some fences to mend. How are you with a hammer?"

42

"Not bad." said Lena. "We lived in a broken-down house for part of my childhood. I helped my father with repairs. But it's been awhile since I wielded a hammer."

"It'll come back fast. Like riding a bike. Muscle memory, you know."

"Mending fences," thought Lena. "If this were Terra, we'd certainly have fences to mend between us."

Lena climbed up beside Lara on the seat of the horse drawn wagon. A trailer behind them was laden with long coal black boards. She could smell the pungent scent of creosote that reminded her of freshly paved roads in her childhood neighborhood back when cars rolled on rubber tires over pavement. Something about that smell felt nostalgic and nearly brought tears to her eyes.

They stopped in front of a section of fence with scattered boards loose from their fence posts. Some were intact, lying at an angle with one end on the ground and the other still attached. Other's had cracked or broken and would need replacing. Lara handed her a hammer and crowbar.

"Start with the broken ones," Lara said. "And pry off the nails from the posts. I'll start fixing the boards that are salvageable."

It took just a few minutes for Lena to get the hang of using the crowbar. As she got into the rhythm of the day's work, she watched Lara lifting boards and swinging her hammer. Her blows were powerful and precise. Three-inch nails were sunk with just one or two swings. And yet, Lena had the impression that she was still holding back.

By the end of an hour, there was a pile of broken boards on the ground and about a dozen spaces in the fencing that would require new boards. Lara instructed her to hold one end in place while she fastened the other end to the post.

Then Lena fastened her end with three nails. It took Lena at least half a dozen blows to sink each nail to the head. By the end of the task, her body was dripping wet, while Lara had barely broken a sweat.

"It's just practice," said Lara, addressing the question in Lena's eyes. "You get used to the rhythm and it gets easier. You did well."

Back at the mess hall, they joined Ellie and Joel at breakfast. As the platters of food were passed, Macklyn crawled up into Ellie's lap and ate from her plate. With the child's head just under the older woman's face, Lena noticed for the first time the resemblance between them. Macklyn was Connor Campbell's biological child and Lily Campbell's grandchild. If Petra Kresky was her biological mother, which parent's genes conferred the Conversion upon the child? And why would they have had the procedure?

"Macklyn's none the worse for wear from her fall yesterday," Lena observed. "She's a remarkable child."

"We're very proud of her," said Joel. "She's quite the acrobat as you've seen. Seems she can do anything she sets her mind to."

"I couldn't help but notice that the cut on her elbow has already healed." Lena risked playing her hand early.

"It's a special herbal concoction," said Ellie without missing a beat. "Some Aloe Vera and a few other magical ingredients. Works every time."

"Must be some magic. I've seen wounds heal that quickly once before, but that was a special child. Her father had undergone a life extending procedure called the Ambrosia Conversion. She'd inherited from him the special properties that it conferred." She glanced at Lara, who avoided her gaze, then noticed Ellie and Joel exchanging looks. She had to be getting close to the truth and only hoped that they wouldn't kick her out before she could confirm her suspicions.

In a moment alone, Lena checked the UDB for the critical dates in the lives of the various pieces of the puzzle she was assembling. Petra Kresky's flight from justice and her disappearance had occurred within days of Terra's death. Given Terra's role in the organization responsible for exchanging consciousness between bodies, it would stand to reason that Terra would have had a similar escape from death at the ready in the course of her dangerous work. And from what Lena understood of the contract between her husband Ray Mettler and Marcus Takana, the host for her identity transfer would likely have undergone the Ambrosia Conversion that would prevent her new body from aging.

Terra's mind in Petra Kresky's body. It was a tantalizing proposition that would explain Macklyn's feats of skill and remarkable powers of healing as well as Lara's strength and apparent imperviousness to the sun's rays. If that was all true, though, then who was Joel? And what was his relationship to this woman and her child?

Lena could barely restrain herself from confronting them all with her conclusions and demanding answers to her lingering questions. But she understood the hazards of exposing what she knew, including the possibility that they wouldn't ever let her leave the compound with their precious secrets. It was, after all, a blockbuster tale that begged to be told, a story that could bring unknown enemies to the Willamette Valley in their pursuit.

9

ABRAHAM BEGAN his rounds just after daybreak. After the previous day's squall and a light rain during the night, the sand underfoot was damp and dense and the fruit on the trees glistened. He started in the groves, where cultivated mango and avocado thrived alongside native breadfruit and banana trees. A few mangoes were showing signs of crimson that promised that they'd soon be sweet. He watched one of his flock cut a ripe breadfruit for their midday meal.

The volcanic soil of the island provided a fertile medium in which all manner of vegetation thrived with a minimum of tending. Abraham walked through a cluster of dozens of knee-high pineapple plants, each bearing a single fruit that would reach a foot or more in height at full maturity. The fruits were still mostly green, but a few were beginning to show signs of yellow peeking between the leaves of the shoots that surrounded the stalk. These would soon be ripe and heavy with juice.

An abundance of vegetables grew from the seeds some of their group had brought to the island. The sea and the tide pools around the shoreline also yielded edible vegetation rich in nutrients. Soon after their arrival, the islanders learned to gather and dry seaweed in solar ovens. There were enough varieties to provide a range of flavors, colors, and nutritional content that was as pleasing to the eye as to the palate. They harvested saltwort, growing thick in the tide pools, to add a salty garnish to various dishes.

The island was too small to domesticate animals and remote enough that bringing breeding stock from the mainland would have been difficult. One of their members became skilled with a slingshot and provided an occasional bird as a delicacy. The heart of their protein source came from the sea. Several of their members collected shellfish in the shallows. Ishmael's skills as a fisherman was responsible for the lion's share of their seafood. His value to their community as a fisherman was rivaled only by his value to the mission as a nanobot engineer and programmer. Abraham considered him one of his most trusted lieutenants, regarding him almost as a son.

Abraham made his way to the beach and rounded a curve to the cove where Ishmael kept his vessels. He often fished from a long, green kayak that was large enough to hold more than a hundred pounds of fish. The kayak was already gone and out of sight. Ishmael must have had an early start that morning and would likely return long before the heat of the noonday sun became treacherous.

The last stop on his morning rounds was the Burning Bush. This was their code name for the electronic brain that would eventually bring back to life the mission that Ganymede had begun before it was raided and lost. Every member of their group was connected to the Universal Data Base via a MELD chip. They each had access to a vast trove of information and digital tools. The flow of data, however, was largely one-way, from the UDB to their brains. Their individual ability to control events in the outside world was limited.

The Burning Bush was designed to communicate with each of their brains and to aggregate the power of their knowledge, augmented by its own ability to learn, into an intelligent entity of astounding capacity. It would eventually have the ability to influence events anywhere in the world, enabling them to revive their network of human subjects, whose brains had been mapped for transfers of consciousness.

The machine was still in its infancy. Some of the basic hardware had been cobbled together from components gathered prior to their retreat to the island. But it required an immense amount of power and meticulous programming that would take years even with their augmented intelligence. The Burning Bush was a combined enterprise that engaged the entire community.

They were still building their power grid from a combination of solar collectors and tidal turbines, constructed largely from plastic and other debris harvested from patches that still floated in the waters among the islands. The volume of debris in the oceans had continued to increase through the early twenties despite ambitious projects to collect it and growing restrictions on products that would eventually wind up in the sea. By mid-century, much of it had been cleared and the ecosystem was beginning to recover from its toxic effects, but enough remained salvageable, turning up after tropical storms, to provide raw materials for the devices of the Lazarus community.

And then there was the wreck. A weather research vessel had sunk in the late thirties, the victim of a waterspout spawned by a storm system the crew had been tracking. It was one of the last such manned expeditions. Abraham's people had discovered it from the air around ten miles out during a drone survey of the area surrounding their island and had sent divers to explore it. It turned out to be a priceless trove of corrosion proof titanium and graphene electronic components that formed the raw materials of the Burning Bush.

When Ishmael had failed to return with his morning's catch by noon, Abraham became concerned. He returned to the beach with binoculars to scan the horizon, but saw no sign of the fisherman. When he pulled up the location of Ishmael's transducer from the UDB, it was nearly forty miles to the southwest, moving on a course toward Tonga.

Abraham felt the blood rise to his face as his fists clenched in anger. Ishmael could have met with an accident or been blown off course by a squall, but he'd already covered a lot of ground for a small hand powered vessel. He briefly considered that Ishmael had been hijacked, but could only conclude that his most trusted lieutenant was making a break for civilization, a betrayal of staggering consequence.

By the time the drone was deployed and circling the area of the signal from Ishmael's transducer, more than two hours had elapsed. There was no sign of the kayak from the air. Abraham guided the tiny drone to within six feet of the water's surface, flying in small circles until he spotted the floating driftwood. As he closed in on it with magnification, he saw the tightly wound turns of fishing line with which Ishmael had fastened the transducer, confirming his worst fear. He'd been betrayed. Not since Terra's treacherous exposure of Ganymede had he been so disappointed.

10

WEEKS PASSED since Natasha's visit to the nerve center at the heart of the hives. She trusted that the music would call her again when it was ready. It played quietly in the background while she navigated her native world.

Thoughts about dolphins and whales also played around the edges of her attention. Their species had all been long endangered, threatened by human activity. The warming and acidification of the seas had posed the most lethal threat, drastically altering the food chain as well as leaving these magnificent creatures vulnerable to a myriad of new parasites and diseases. Ironically, the rising seas, also an effect of global warming, diluted some of the more toxic chemical threats in the water and disrupted the development of coastal communities enough to diminish the rate of commercial fishing, reduce wastewater effluent along the coasts, and allow nature to begin to restore some of the native coastal habitats, such as mangroves and corals, essential to the breeding of a diversity of sea life.

Natasha burned with curiosity about how her newfound abilities would enable her to interact with the mammals of the sea. Where might she go to test these abilities and how would she get there? How strange that she'd been able to visit another dimension without leaving her home, but to find dolphins in the Atlantic she'd need tickets to ride. There were still a few places along the Florida coast frequented by dolphins. Manatees had long since vanished entirely despite valiant efforts by conservationists to save them. And as parts of Florida became inundated by rising tides, the Georgia and Carolina coasts, which had also shifted westward, enjoyed both warmer weather and seas that were hospitable to tropical species. As barrier islands became permanently submerged, the man-made structures upon them became the foundations for vast reefs that supported new life to restart the food chain at the microscopic level. Given a chance, life finds a way.

"But what of the dolphin-like creatures in the other world?" Natasha wondered. How did they fare with the environmental catastrophe that had driven the people inside the hives? She realized that she'd seen no sign of them among the life teeming just beyond the hives. Had they survived at all? She felt certain that the people of that world would have done everything possible to save them, but they may have had all they could do just to save themselves.

Natasha pulled up the schedule of the vacuum tube transport from the District of Columbia to points south and bought a ticket to Savannah. From the time her capsule left the station, it was less than half an hour to her destination, acceleration and deceleration accounting for most of that time. She arrived in a city carved by canals that divided it into a network of islands connected by a vast web of bridges. On some of the islands were clusters of Victorian mansions, remnants of the city's former glory, while on others were neighborhoods of modular homes built on sturdy wooden stilts or concrete piers that kept the living areas high and dry. Further inland, beyond the reach of the waters were hospitals and other infrastructure crucial to the community's welfare.

She would explore the wonders of this historic city by night, but her primary mission here was offshore. She rented a skiff and some snorkeling gear and was upon the water at daybreak. It was a glorious day, the sun rising slowly through the mist on the horizon, a great red orb that reflected upon the water and cast streaks of orange and pink across the azure background of the sky. There was still a cool breeze, but the heat would soon become oppressive as the sun rose further into the sky and sent its relentless radiation earthward. Soon enough, though, she'd be shielded from the heated air by the ocean, which was still comfortably below body temperature.

How far would she have to venture from shore to find her quarry? She wasn't sure that she would find them at all. Their numbers were so few and they no longer frequented the shoreline. Like looking for needles in a vast wet haystack. But these needles weren't silent. They emitted pulses of energy that she was now specially equipped to detect. At least she hoped she was. That's what she was there to learn.

Miles out, she found a shoal that had once been an island and dropped anchor. She donned her fins, mask, and snorkel and slipped over the gunwale into the water. How clumsy her gear felt compared with the sleek and agile body she'd possessed in the other world that was so perfectly adapted for living underwater. The snorkel kept her bound closely to the surface most of the time. She could dive and hold her breath for four or five minutes, far longer than most people, because of the unique qualities of the body she possessed in this world, but she still had to surface from time to time to breathe. She'd chosen not to use Scuba gear in order to minimize the barrier between her body and the water so that she could make optimal use of her senses, especially the newest one that was mediated by her skin.

Natasha stood vertically in the water and let herself drift into the depth in much the same way that she had during her first voyage to the other dimension. She was able to settle to stillness, the weight of her body perfectly balanced by the buoyancy of the water, and waited, eyes closed, her silence undisturbed by breath. Then she heard the first faint ping, followed by another and another, the pitch of the sounds rising, telling her that their source was moving toward her.

When she opened her eyes, she was surrounded on all sides by powerful creatures moving as one in a circle around her. And then she noticed another sound, deeper, and rhythmic, also coming from the ring of dolphins. It was a reflected pulse and its origin was her own body. She had joined the conversation and they were treating her as one of their own. It made little difference what the conversation was about.

As the dolphins circled, the rhythmic sound of her own Sonar's reflections became the dominant note until she noticed the strains of the music rising in the background.

"Now?" she thought, but knew she could do nothing but go with the flow. The images of the dolphins faded, the water became murky, and endless columns of hives rose from the ocean floor almost to the surface far above her, encompassing her, protecting her, giving her life. The mask and fins were gone. She was still without breath, but no longer holding it. She was home.

Each time she visited the world of the creators, it became more familiar while at the same time transformed compared with the last visit. Now the geography of their world had changed, with another primarily vertical expansion of the hives as well as a contraction of the clear viable perimeter around them. But the more striking change was internal: a new and disquieting sensation in her belly unfamiliar to her in her experience in either of her worlds. It was gnawing hunger...no, beyond hunger, starvation.

As she looked around at her companions of this era, in place of the naturally slender and fit forms that she'd previously encountered were withered beings, anguish etching faces that generations ago had been smooth and serene. And as their collective desperation accumulated within her, it seemed almost unbearable. For the first time, she wondered whether she would survive her stay upon this world and ever see home again.

She was drawn again to the nerve center within the hives, which was surrounded as before by people at stations, gesturing with bony fingers as they interacted with it. In place of a single ring of operators, however, was a vertical array, a dozen high, around the central column. As she glided around the array of bodies, around the middle level was one empty station. She assumed her place in the network and let her fingers join the dance.

As the funnel of energy formed and spun before her, she noticed something new materialize at the top of the column. It was a capsule, much like the capsule in which she'd ridden in the vacuum tube transport, rising atop the column toward the surface. And as the capsule accelerated, she found herself lying between its two passengers, seeing what they saw and feeling what they felt.

They were moving toward a light. At first it was the familiar green orb that had shone through layer upon layer of water when it had been pristine and transparent. As they continued toward the surface, its color faded to a yellowish tinge, then feathered to orange, then red, and finally scarlet, with shimmering reflected images receding around them across the approaching interface between liquid and atmosphere. Then it dawned on her that this was unexplored territory. They were scouts, the first ever to visit the surface of their planet. And they had no idea what lied above.

When the capsule crashed through the surface, it rotated to a horizontal position and plowed through the water toward something in the distance that Natasha recognized as land, but was entirely alien to her companions. Soon after they surfaced, however, the blistering heat of the atmosphere began to take its toll. The shell of the capsule was designed to withstand extremes of temperature, but its inventors had underestimated the intensity of the sun's rays, unfiltered by many fathoms of water. The longer they were on the surface, the hotter the interior of the capsule became. The capsule's shell finally began to melt and she watched her companions succumb to the stifling heat. Then she felt herself spinning.

The capsule was gone. She was lying just on the surface of the water, going round and round, borne atop the ring of dolphins that were enabling her to breathe air, keeping safe the body she'd left behind while she'd leapt to another dimension. Then they began to slip away, letting her gently into the water. As she floated face down on the surface, she heard the pitch of the pings deepen as her saviors receded. And for just a moment, she imagined she heard laughter.

11

LENA HAD SHOWERED and was just about to get into bed for the night when there was a knock on the door. She opened it. Ellie stood before her.

"Can I come in?" asked Ellie, as if she needed permission. "We should talk."

Lena invited her in. Ellie sat on the bed and invited Lena to sit beside her.

"I've been watching you," Ellie began, "and have come to several conclusions. First, I sense that your age and experience has brought considerable wisdom and discretion."

Lena bid her silently to go on.

"Second, I think I can trust you to appreciate the jeopardy that you could bring to our community and to respect our need for security." She paused. "You and I have most of our lives behind us, but as you can see, most of our people are still at the beginnings of their lives and have much to lose."

Lena nodded. While there were still mysteries about these people, she'd learned enough about them to value their survival.

"And finally," Ellie continued, "you are a skilled journalist with a keen eye for detail. I expect you already know too many of our secrets. So we're going to have to trust each other."

"I can't imagine," Lena began after considering where to start, "the pain you and your people have been through. I'm so sorry for the loss of your son." She held out her hand. Ellie took it and smiled as a single tear rolled down her cheek.

"So you know part of our story," said Ellie. "You must want to know the rest of it. This is where your discretion and wisdom, and your compassion, come in."

Lena nodded and waited for Ellie to continue.

"As you've already gathered, my real name is Lily Campbell. Together with my son Connor, I led Mandala, a community of farmers that settled in Maryland. You know about the massacre that took a dozen of our members. And you know that Connor was named as the killer, presumably having suddenly gone mad."

"And you had to shoot him to keep him from killing others," added Lena. "That must have been agonizing."

"It was, but what you don't know is that it wasn't really Connor. I'd guessed it before I shot him, or I might not have been able to do it."

"I don't understand. If not Connor, then who? And how?"

"His name was Ethan, He was an operative of a clandestine government unit called Ganymede that was behind the rash of identity exchanges that occurred five years ago. They had developed a technology to exchange consciousness between bodies, which they planned eventually to use to control governments around the world, including ours."

"So Ethan took over Connor's body and killed your people," concluded Lena. "But why?"

"Because we were more than farmers. Ganymede's technology threatened the natural order of things, the circle of life. We dedicated ourselves to sabotaging their plan.

Connor and several others were highly skilled hackers, who managed to interfere with their network and trigger exchanges before Ganymede had intended for them to occur."

"Then this was revenge?"

"Yes, against us, especially Connor, and against Terra, whom you know as Lara. Ethan was about to kill Terra when I shot him."

"Terra," said Lena. "Then I was right. I watched her die."

Ellie gasped. Terra had told her that she and Lena had crossed paths in her previous life, but had not provided all the details. That Lena had witnessed her death came as a shock.

"She was protecting Marcus Takana and my husband Ray," Lena continued. "That scene is still a vivid memory. Ray died in an accident later that day."

"It seems we've all been touched with tragedy," said Ellie, "and all in some way at the hands of Ganymede."

"So it's all beginning to make sense. Terra's mind took over Petra Kresky's body. Macklyn is the biological daughter of Petra Kresky and your son Connor. But if Ethan died in Connor's body, what happened to Connor?" Lena already had an inkling of the answer.

"Ethan had already taken over another body, a lumberjack named Tobias Batie. Connor wound up in his body and we managed to rescue him in the raid on Ganymede."

"Then Joel is Connor," Lena concluded, "as I suspected. So where do we go from here?"

"Ganymede is still a threat," said Ellie. "When Terra led a raid on their headquarters to rescue Connor, they all committed suicide with cyanide rather than be captured. But every Ganymede operative bore a transducer that mapped their brains to young healthy hosts, all of whom have had the Ambrosia Conversion. When their bodies died, they acquired new identities in eternally young bodies. We expect them to regroup."

"Regroup? To what end?"

"To resume their quest for world domination. And to learn as much as possible about the capabilities of their new bodies," replied Ellie. "They'd only had a chance to observe the effects in others. Now they're experiencing them first hand. And there's a lot left to discover. For example, what happens to their offspring?"

"Like Natasha Takana," said Lena, "and Macklyn."

"Exactly. We expect them eventually to come after both girls. If they can get their hands on them, there's no telling how they might go about studying them. We need to do everything possible to keep them safe."

"They'd have no trouble locating Natasha," added Lena, "but Marcus and his family would have tight security. How would they find you?"

"If you found us, they can, too. They're a highly skilled clandestine unit, after all. They can find anyone they want. And they would also want to find Terra. In their eyes, she was a traitor. Her betrayal would be unforgivable in their eyes."

Lena's thoughts went back to Terra's first intrusion into her life. She was, after all, responsible for getting Ray involved in the contract that ultimately led to his death. Lena's first impression was of a devil. And back then Terra was still loyal to Ganymede, an agent of an evil machine. But

Lara...she was something else altogether. Human, likeable, caring, drastically transformed. Could she really be trusted? And could she ever be forgiven?

12

BY THE TIME ISHMAEL awoke, the sun had dipped halfway to the horizon in the west. He was already beginning to feel hungry and was grateful for the remnants of the morning's meal that surrounded the solar cooker. He scooped a handful of breadfruit, but ate sparingly. A too full stomach could become a liability once back on the open sea. He packed some of the remaining food for the next leg of the journey.

He would start the journey while it was still daylight and paddle through the night. The first few hours would be risky. He was still within range of Abraham's drones. By now, Abraham would have discovered his flight and the search would be on. But, hopefully, his diversion had worked and bought him time before Abraham would be on his trail. He scanned the horizon before dragging the kayak back to the beach.

Around a quarter mile off the beach, Ishmael felt the pull of the northwesterly current and aligned the bow of his craft with it. He pulled the paddle in a steady rhythm, left, then right, lifting the ends of the paddle just clear of the water, then dipping them just below the surface to join the current propelling him forward. The rhythm of the work along with the gliding motion of the kayak and the glittering reflection of the sun on the water's surface was hypnotic. He was hardly aware of the passage of time or the miles he traversed. Only the relentless march of the sun toward the horizon marked his progress.

The sun fell against a cloudless sky until extinguishing itself in the sea. Ishmael thought he saw a brief flash of green on the horizon the moment the sun disappeared. The water soon turned dark. Then the last flickers of color in the sky were swallowed by the curtain that rose from the sea.

Ishmael was at home on the sea under the cloak of darkness. The current was steady and true. He could easily stay on course even without navigating by the satellites that communicated with his MELD chip. The biggest challenge would be the selection of the next stepping stone in his island-hopping journey from the many possibilities on the way toward Samoa. A measure of randomness in his course would help him evade pursuit.

It was a moonless night. For the first several hours, the sky was filled with the twinkle of starlight from horizon to horizon, while the craggy swath of the Milky Way crept across the sky until the bright galactic center was almost overhead. By midnight, clouds had rolled in, obscuring all but a scattering of stars, turning the world around Ishmael pitch black. He could no longer even see the outline of the kayak directly in front of him. The rhythm of the paddle pulling him through the water kept him on task.

In the early morning hours, still in total darkness, the kayak was jolted by a collision with something unseen. The obstruction flexed enough to absorb some of the initial shock of impact, then pulled the vessel into its orbit, rotating slowly in a wide circle as it forged ahead in the current. The ends of Ishmael's paddle could no longer find purchase in the water, striking a layer of semi-solid material on its surface.

There was nothing he could do. He laid back in the kayak and went with the flow, turning lazy circles as he drifted toward his destination. Hours later, as the light began to break across the horizon, Ishmael caught the first glimpse of what had captured him. He was surrounded by a garbage patch of plastic that extended in all directions almost as far as the eye could see. The island of debris was a multicolored mess of bottles, bags, and random loops and swirls that obscured the boundaries of the kayak, now blended seamlessly with its surroundings.

Ishmael let the floating mass carry him along while plotting how he would break free from its grasp once near his destination. He was in no hurry to work the paddle as long he was drifting in the right direction. He was just ten miles away from the next island in his aquatic game of hopscotch. The patch made steady progress forward while it rotated slowly counterclockwise.

Around mid-morning, he was distracted by a whirring sound behind him. Turning he saw the tiny drone a hundred yards away and around twenty yards above the water, rapidly closing the gap between them. He crouched in the kayak in a fetal position, making his body as small as possible. The drone swooped closer to the water, passing wide to starboard, and vanished in the distance ahead.

Why hadn't it flown directly overhead for a clearer look? And why didn't it circle back? Could it possibly have missed him from such close quarters? There was no way to know for sure. But the serendipitous presence of the multicolored swath of plastic may have provided sufficient camouflage to hide Ishmael and his vessel from the camera. If not, he could expect Abraham's hovercraft to appear in short order to bring him back as a captive to the island colony or to kill him.

It was time to break free and make a run for the next island where he could find cover until dark. How could he persuade the floating mass around him to release its prey? If he could create enough of a break in the mass off his bow to let in a stream of water, the rotation might push the leading edge away and unwind the spiral, exposing a clear path to open water.

He would need to initiate the opening at the leading edge of the plastic island. That would mean risking separating himself from his craft and rejoining it before it floated free.

63

Ishmael donned a pair of swim fins to distribute his weight atop the fragile surface of the floating island, grabbed the gaff that he used to pull fish aboard his boat, and set off gingerly on foot ahead of the bow. The surface supported his weight. It took a few minutes for him to adjust to the rotation and steady his balance. Then he moved with ease toward the edge.

The challenge would be to find the exact place on the perimeter of the circular mass to start the opening that would take into account its rate of rotation so that the resulting arc would terminate at the bow of the kayak. With the augmented intelligence conferred by his MELD chip, the math would be easy. He located the inception point 68 degrees to the left of center and made his way to that point on the boundary. Once there, he dug the point of the gaff into the mass of plastic and pulled it parallel to the circumference. The mass parted slightly. He worked his way with the gaff quickly toward the center, creating a sliver of an opening that widened naturally from the outside as the rotation sheared the left side of the mass away from the right in a perfect parabola.

By the time he approached the kayak at the center, the swirling gyre was doing all the work opening the passage. The boat began to wriggle free, then suddenly shot forward. It was moving too fast to intercept it on foot. Ishmael dove into the water and kicked as hard as he could toward the path of the kayak. He caught up to it just as it floated past, reached out with the gaff and hooked the stern in the nick of time, pulling himself alongside and rolling over the gunwale into the boat. By the time he was aboard, it was gliding steadily with the current, free of the plastic tangle.

The sun was getting high. The water evaporating from his skin cooled him momentarily, but soon the heat was relentless. A volcanic peak came into view over the horizon, the distance closing rapidly before his eyes. According to his navigational data, this was precisely the island he'd chosen for his next destination. Incredible luck!

Once ashore, fresh water wasn't far away. This island was as much a tropical paradise as the last, replete with waterfalls and trees laden with ripe fruit. Hiding the boat was an immediate priority, given his recent encounter with one of Abraham's drones. The next encounter, if there was one, might not be as lucky as the first.

Time was now of the essence. Ishmael could no longer afford his painstaking route from island to island. He needed a swifter passage to civilization along with sufficient stealth to evade detection both from Abraham's drones and from satellite surveillance. It was time to use some of Dev Renner's resources that he'd retrieved prior to his departure from Abraham's island.

Ishmael logged onto the Dark Web and searched for submersible drones. He was looking specifically for a novel type of vessel that simulated the form and motion of sharks. These came in sizes that could hold up to three passengers and moved in a powerful kinetic pattern that was virtually indistinguishable from a shark and undetectable especially when traveling within a natural school.

He found what he was looking for and placed his order, providing his current coordinates and releasing the required payment from one of his hidden cryptocurrency wallets. His ride would come from Samoa and be there by morning. Powered by nuclear fusion, its range was thousands of miles and could take him straight to New Zealand, Australia, or Japan.

Since Abraham would likely anticipate his arrival in Samoa and be waiting for him there, a direct break for the mainland would be his best chance to complete his escape from Lazarus. Now he could only hope that his transaction went through and that the submersible would arrive undetected. There was nothing left to do but sleep.

13

BY THE TIME NATASHA clambered aboard her skiff and made for shore, night was beginning to fall. Cottony clouds hung above the horizon, illuminated with streaks of vermilion and accented with azure patches in the spaces between. The setting sun behind the clouds projected its glow above them to the cloudless part of the sky, casting orange and scarlet reflections on the water's surface. When the sun had finished setting, the seas turned dark against the twilit sky until the darkness rose to fill the rest of the universe.

Natasha was returning with more than she'd sought on this voyage of exploration. She'd confirmed her newfound gifts and had made intelligent first contact with dolphins. And she'd also learned more about the fate of the Creators. Their environment had become fouled to an apparently hopeless extent. They were running out of resources, facing starvation, and seeking possible escape from their watery world to their planet's surface. But their first foray was doomed. The atmosphere of this planet seemed incompatible with life. And even with their advanced technology, they were unlikely to find a way to colonize the surface in time to save themselves.

If their civilization perished, then who wrote the DNA code that was responsible for summoning her to their world and perhaps for life on earth? Would that be the last of her contact with them or would they find a way to tell the rest of their story? Natasha could still feel the emptiness in her belly that she felt while dwelling in the hives. Here, at least, she'd be able to slake her hunger. She was not about to die.

Natasha rode the last run of the night on the vacuum tube transport and was home by midnight. For just a moment aboard the train, she'd begun to feel heat radiating from the shell of her compartment and imagined that she was back aboard the ill-fated capsule in the other world, but the feeling had passed and she arrived at her destination unscathed.

As she approached her house, she saw lights flashing in the distance. As she got closer, she saw an ambulance parked in the driveway. Emergency personnel were wheeling a stretcher from the open front door with a person lying motionless upon it. When she was close enough to make out the identity of the passenger, her breath stopped short, stifling a scream. It was Corinne.

Her father stood beside the stretcher looking frazzled. He'd always been calm in the face of any other threat. It was unsettling for her to see him looking so distraught. She ran from the car to his side and grasped his hand. He put his other hand on top of hers and mustered a weak smile.

"What happened?" asked Natasha.

"Your mother's been very ill," answered Marcus. "We haven't wanted to worry you, but it's time you knew."

"Is she going to die?"

"Not now...at least I don't think so. But I don't know how much time she has."

Corinne stirred. Her face looked dusky and she struggled for breath. An EMT put a mask over her face. Her breathing slowed and became regular and color returned to her face. Her eyes opened slightly. Natasha reached with her free hand and took Corinne's.

"I don't understand," said Natasha. "Most diseases have been wiped out. People are living way past 100. What's happened to her?"

"That's partly why we've kept this from you," replied Marcus. "As you know, when you were conceived, I'd had the Ambrosia Conversion to stop me from aging and half of your genes came from me. Nobody had any idea what the consequences of that might be. Fortunately, you were born healthy...better than healthy." He paused and sighed deeply. "But your mother didn't fare as well. Your heightened metabolism made tremendous demands on her body and weakened some of her organs. The effects were imperceptible at first, but over the years her body has aged faster than normal."

"Then it was my fault," concluded Natasha, choking back tears.

"No, Sweetie, not your fault. You didn't choose to be born. If anything, it was my fault for keeping my condition secret from your mother. She was livid when she found out that I'd had the Conversion. But we both agree that we wouldn't change anything. You're the best thing that ever happened to us."

Natasha let her father's words sink in. She was grateful for them, but still felt responsible, like a parasite that had sucked some of the life out of the mother she adored.

"So what is it that's killing her?"

"The pregnancy also weakened her immune system. You were genetically different from an ordinary fetus. Her body saw you as an invader and mounted an immune response against you. You were fortunately strong enough to resist the assault. But the response left her immunity compromised. She's been susceptible to infections that no longer threaten others. We've had to bring back some of the antibiotics that were used decades ago, but she's become resistant to most of them."

"Is there anything else we can do?" asked Natasha.

"No...nothing," said Marcus, averting his eyes.

Natasha picked up on his avoidance of her gaze. Why was he lying to her?

"There's something I can do. Isn't there?" she said at last. Then she understood. She'd learned about studies in the early part of the century on parabiosis...hooking up the circulations of old animals to young animals. The effect was distinct from the effect of simple transfusions. It had turned back the aging clock on the elderly subjects, but at the expense of advancing the age of the younger ones. The molecular components responsible for this effect had been isolated and resulted in drugs that slowed aging. But perhaps parabiosis was a way to reverse Corinne's unique vulnerabilities. Perhaps Natasha's blood held the antidote.

"We'd considered it," Marcus said, reading in her eyes that she'd figured it out, "but your mother would have none of it. She didn't want to risk your health...or your life. But she's also been a stickler for letting nature take its course. That's why she didn't have the Conversion after I'd urged her to have it. And that's why I agreed to have it reversed."

Corinne was loaded into the ambulance and it was on its way. Natasha watched it recede into the distance as the pitch of its pulsating siren fell, reminding her of the departing dolphins just a few hours before.

So much had happened since she'd last slept. So much loss. So much misery. She'd watched an entire civilization dying and was powerless to help. Now her beloved mother was dying and she still felt powerless. The one thing she could do, her mother wasn't going to permit. There had to be something. There just had to be.

14

ISHMAEL'S SLUMBER was still and dreamless. He was exhausted by his journey and his struggle to free himself from the plastic garbage patch. His extraordinary body, however, recovered full strength by morning and was ready for the next leg of his escape. He awoke just before dawn to a tactile notification that his ride had arrived.

As he opened his eyes the sun was just poking its leading edge above the horizon to the east. The sky was illuminated with a dazzling display of colored light scattered by the feathery clouds that floated over the sea. He scanned the shoreline for the vessel, but saw only waves rolling toward the beach and gently breaking in their regular rhythm.

Ishmael searched for a message from his supplier within his encrypted inbox in the cloud and found what he was looking for: the dedicated frequency and passkey to control the submersible. He waded into the surf, striding through the breaking waves. He was neck deep when he passed the point where the waves were beginning to form. The surface of the water still ahead was smooth.

Looking below the surface, he spotted a moving shadow, plunged his head under water and glided toward it. As he got closer, the shadow gradually took shape and came into focus. A huge shark now loomed within striking distance, swimming in small circles, its body undulating with the powerful strokes of its tail. Then it appeared to see him and widened the circles to surround its newfound prey. Ishmael smiled.

With the power of his MELD chip, he engaged the frequency provided in the message and transmitted the passkey. The shark stopped circling, gliding obediently to his side, then followed him as he moved back through the waves toward the beach. He left it submerged in four feet of water and returned to land. He would need to find a way to board before bringing it to the surface.

He pulled up a satellite view of the island, zooming in to see the topography of the surrounding waters. Just off the western shore was a ledge extending out fifty feet at a depth of just a foot or two, then dropping suddenly to twenty feet. This would be his makeshift dock. In daylight, he would need to act quickly to escape detection by Abraham's drones. A few minutes on the surface was all he could risk.

It took less than an hour for Ishmael to cross the island, bringing with him just enough food for the trip and the limited gear that would fit within the compact module. He would buy whatever else he needed when he reached civilization. Staying hidden in the trees, he summoned the submersible and tracked its progress around the island. When it was directly in front of him, he walked into the ankle-deep water and commanded the craft to surface. He arrived at the drop-off just as it topped the water. Upon his command, a hatch on top opened. He scrambled in, the hatch closed, and the craft submerged. The whole operation, from the time the craft broke the surface to the time it disappeared back into the depths, took less than four minutes. No drones had appeared in the sky. Ishmael felt confident that he was so far undetected.

As the submersible slipped away from the island into open water, it attracted the attention of a school of sharks that soon surrounded it.

"Good," thought Ishmael. "That was easier than I expected." He activated the sonar that enabled the shark drone to assume its position within the school and maintain the proper distance from its companions. The camouflage was complete and hopefully coordinated precisely enough to evade detection. The school was headed westward. He would stay with the school as long as it was headed in the right direction, then navigate toward the coast of Australia.

In his previous life, Ishmael had once swum with sharks for the thrill of it. Sharing their space and their surging power had been an otherworldly experience that removed him from the cares of the world above the water's surface. He'd never felt so free. Now he was being propelled in a pattern identical to that of the creatures surrounding him, which felt almost like being one of them. At least for the moment, Lazarus became a distant memory, shrouded in fog.

Lost within the pulsing rush of primitive creatures, Ishmael's reverie was broken by the hum of a motor coming from behind him and gaining fast. He scrolled through the camera images on his monitor until he spotted an object moving low above the water's surface in pursuit. As the object came into focus, he recognized it as one of Abraham's drones. Had it penetrated his disguise, or had it simply been attracted by the massive disturbance created by the school?

The drone swooped directly overhead, then fell back just far enough to get him in its sights. Ishmael saw a flash from the front of the aircraft, then a projectile cutting through the water, headed straight for him and closing in fast. He heard an explosion and the submersible shook. He waited for the rush of water to fill the vessel and envelop him. It never came.

The carcass of a shark just off his bow plunged toward the ocean floor, a gaping hole in its tail, leaving a long trail of blood. The school never lost its rhythm, the submersible keeping pace all the way. The drone faded back into the distance until it could no longer be seen or heard.

Ishmael knew Abraham's drones' capabilities because he'd done most of their programming. He knew that their artificial intelligence had been trained to recognize patterns and to pick out anomalies of shape, color, or movement of objects that didn't fit perfectly with their surroundings. He had done his job well and should have been dead. So what had gone wrong?

Whoever designed the submersible had done their job even better. It had mimicked the behavior of the schooling sharks so well, in fact, that an inadvertent wobble in the course of one of its living companions identified it as the outlier and targeted the unfortunate creature for destruction.

Hours later, the school turned northward and Ishmael broke from the pack continuing to head due west. The submersible dropped another forty feet into the depths, accelerating to an astonishing speed for a watercraft. By noon the following day, he was closing in on the Australian coast. The vessel slowed as the water became shallower, rising to glide across the outer reaches of the Great Barrier Reef.

The submersible's monitors now displayed a panorama of delicate structures, including stalagmite like pillars, branching forms, intricately etched forms that seemed to mimic human brains, and exquisite filigrees. Much of the panorama was painted with dazzling iridescent color, set off by equally brilliant fish darting in and out of the crevices in the structure. But substantial patches were bleached stark white and devoid of the life forms that lived symbiotically with the reef.

Ishmael remembered swimming as a very small child long, long ago over a reef vibrant in color as far as the eye could see. Years later, he'd revisited the spot, only to find a vast expanse of chalky white skeleton, the remains of the reef that had been ravaged by changes in the temperature and acidity of the surrounding ocean. With meticulous nurturing by marine scientists, new strains of corals had subsequently been planted that were better adapted to the changing environment and the reefs were coming back to life. He was now observing an ecosystem in transition back to health.

Another hour and the vessel was in Port Douglas. It surfaced just before approaching the dock and pulled alongside. Ishmael emerged to find a crowd of curious tourists admiring his bizarre conveyance and hurried quickly ashore after dispatching the drone back to its owners. The last thing he wanted was attention.

Now that he was back in civilization, evading detection would bring a new level of complexity. There would be cameras everywhere that were capable of recognizing even well-disguised faces. Abraham was unlikely to find him there in real time, partly because he'd have little idea where to look, but mainly because Ishmael had sabotaged Lazarus's digital command center and the community would be scrambling to repair its electronic infrastructure. He'd also planted a virus in the Burning Bush that would eventually obliterate its programs.

"It'll take them weeks to recover," Ishmael thought. The monkey wrench he'd thrown into their digital world would create extensive damage. Repairing it would be further complicated by the absence of the devices' chief architect. Ishmael's skills as a fisherman had been invaluable to the community, but his technical skills were indispensable.

Even so, the ever-present surveillance in the city streets would record his movements and create a trail that Abraham might follow once he figured out where Ishmael had made landfall. He would need to move quickly and spend as little time as possible in public places. And public transportation like the vacuum tube transport was out of the question. Even a taxi or hailed ride would create a record of his movements.

Standing in the shadows outside a coffee shop, he watched people come and go, observing everything from their mood and clothing to the tempo of their movements. He settled upon a casually dressed, clean-shaven young man, who appeared relaxed and had lingered longer than most of the other customers, then followed him to his car.

"Excuse me, sir," said Ishmael, "Could you do me a favor?"

The man looked at him with suspicion and ducked into the driver's seat without replying. He began to close the door.

"I can make it well worth your while," added Ishmael, stopping the door with the heel of his left hand. "Please hear me out."

The man thought a moment, then released his hold on the door handle, avoiding a physical confrontation.

"I'll pay you a thousand dollars to drive me to the Cairns Airport," Ishmael said, flashing a roll of currency.

The man's eyes got wide. Very few transactions still occurred with currency and its rarity had added a premium to its value. This was quite a lot of money for an hour's drive. Ishmael waited patiently as the young man mulled his offer.

"Right, Mate. Get in," he said at last, opening the passenger side door.

Ishmael walked around and took the shotgun seat. The driver touched a screen and the door closed and locked. Then Ishmael heard the quiet hum of the electric motor as the car slid into traffic. He did not encourage conversation and the driver seemed content to proceed in silence, permitting Ishmael time to complete his next pressing task.

Accessing the UDB with his thoughts, he found one of the smaller air charter companies that operated out of Cairns and chartered the smallest jet in its fleet. It would be waiting for him in a private hangar. Then he pulled up a satellite map and entered the coordinates he remembered for Mandala's compound in the Maryland countryside. He watched as the image zoomed in from space. The outline of North America disappeared around the edges as the details of the topography began to come into focus. The cityscapes of Washington and Baltimore appeared, then moved to the periphery and disappeared from the edge. When the image finally came to rest, all he could see was pasture and scrub vegetation. There wasn't a sign that anyone had ever lived there.

Ishmael shook his head in surprise, reentered the coordinates, and got the same result. He then scanned a twenty-five mile radius and found no signs of a settlement. What had become of them? And what had become of Terra?

Terra had been crucial to the next phase of Ishmael's plan. They had enjoyed a mutually respectful relationship back in their days together at Ganymede and he believed that he could trust her again now. She'd been one of their most resourceful operatives. Together they would have a better chance of evading Lazarus than either of them would alone.

He next pulled up images of Petra Kresky and Tobias Batie from the UDB and searched for them in real time, coming up empty. They were well-hidden from the prying eyes of civilization. He then rolled the timeline backward until they showed up. They finally surfaced four years earlier in the town of Cottage Grove, Oregon at a farming supply store. Terra had made some changes to the appearance of her host. Her hair was dirty blond and tied back in a ponytail. Her eyes were back to Petra's native hazel color. She'd removed the green contact lenses she'd fashioned when she'd resumed her identity as Terra. The appearance of Connor Campbell's host looked largely unchanged. Running the timeline forward again, he watched them leave the town limits to the west and disappear from view forever.

"So they're somewhere in the Willamette Valley," he concluded. "Looks like I'm headed to Oregon."

The airport appeared in the distance. Ishmael directed the driver to a side road on the perimeter of the airfield. A gate opened and they pulled up to a hangar. He handed the driver the roll of bills, which actually held twice the sum he'd promised, and waved him off, then entered the hangar from a side door.

Inside was a sleek twin engine jet about as tall as he was, its door open just three steps above the ground, a two seater no bigger than a Viper, but a hell of lot faster. The pilot stood by the stairway and invited him inside. When the pilot had assumed his position in the cockpit, he looked to Ishmael for instructions.

"Eugene Oregon," said Ishmael, "and we're flying in stealth mode. No flight plan."

The pilot nodded his assent and smiled. Even more than he loved flying, he loved flying cloak and dagger missions. And he knew that discretion meant never asking his passengers' identities.

Ishmael leaned back and closed his eyes. The aircraft rolled out of the hangar and onto the nearest runway and was airborne within minutes. He had high hopes of finding Terra at the other end of his journey. What he would do when he found her he had not yet worked out.

15

ELLIE WAS LINGERING over her mid-morning coffee when one of the sentries burst into the cafe.

"Someone's approaching," announced the man, catching his breath, "on horseback."

Ripples spread across the previously smooth surface of the liquid toward the rim of the cup. Ellie wasn't easily rattled, but this was the second intruder at their sanctuary in just a few weeks after years of maintaining utter secrecy. The first had been Lena, who now enjoyed a trusted position within the community. So who was this other stranger? And could Lena have alerted him to their presence? Was she not to be trusted, after all?

"Man or woman?" Ellie asked.

"Looked pretty tall," said the sentry. "Best I could tell a man. He was still pretty far away."

They emerged from the cafe, got into a horse drawn cart, and rode out to the stockade. As they came to a halt, they could hear the sound of hoofbeats coming from the other side of the main gates. Then the galloping stopped.

"Who goes there?" called a rifleman from atop the barricade.

"My name is Dev," replied the stranger in a resonant voice from the other side of the gates.

"What do you want?"

"I have a proposition for you. An offer of considerable value that you might not want to refuse."

"Strangers aren't welcome around here."

"I know," answered the man, "but as you can see, I've found you. And others will be looking for you. I just might be able to help you hold them off."

The rifleman looked behind him at Ellie, who gestured for him to let the man inside.

The gates creaked open. In trotted a handsome Paint carrying a wiry looking man in his early twenties. The man was fair skinned with sandy hair and a well-trimmed sandy moustache that framed the corners of his mouth. He was dressed in jeans and a denim long sleeved shirt, two-toned Western boots, and a red bandanna, all of which appeared brand new. He looked like a city slicker masquerading as a cowboy. A canvas pack slung just behind the saddle contained whatever meagre possessions he'd brought with him. The horse came to a halt just fifteen yards in front of Ellie, who now stood with feet planted wide and hands on hips. The stranger dismounted.

"Who are you?" Ellie asked, "and what are you doing on our property?"

"My name is Dev Renner," replied Ishmael, "and I'm a hacker like you and your people."

That caught Ellie off balance. This stranger knew way too much already and could only be trouble.

"And like you," Ishmael continued when he'd gauged that she was ready for more information, "I'm on the run and looking for a place to hide."

Ellie thought a while before responding. If he were truly on the run, then there must be people on his trail, which made his presence dangerous.

"Who's after you?" she asked, "and why?"

"Like I said, I'm a hacker," Ishmael answered, "and I've done some things in the investment world that, shall we say, has left a lot of people not very happy with me. My gains have been their losses."

"Then what's going to keep them from finding you here?"

"I've managed to fall off the radar for a long time. I've always stayed a few steps ahead of my pursuers. But I've done that by isolating myself from the world. It's time for some human contact. So I came here."

"Then why us?" Ellie asked. "You could have gone anywhere."

"Because you've also managed to stay off the grid. And because I think I can be useful to you. I'm very skilled at what I do."

"Hacking…"

"Yes, hacking."

Ellie's instincts told her that there was much more to this man's story and motives that he was not telling her, but she was curious about what exactly he had to offer. They would have to watch him closely, but it wouldn't hurt to find out more.

"We can talk," she said at last. "Follow me." She got back in the cart and headed toward the cafe. Ishmael remounted the Paint and followed. By the time they reached town, a crowd had gathered and watched them approach. Joel and

Lara stood just inside the door of the cafe. Lena was seated inside.

Once inside, Ellie introduced Dev Renner to the others. Lena used her MELD chip to run a quick scan of his face and search the UDB. She got an instant hit on Dev Renner, a reclusive genius who had reputedly used cunning to strike it rich, then seemed to disappear off the face of the earth. The UDB showed no traces of his existence for nearly five years. And suddenly, here he was.

Lena caught Ellie's eye and nodded, confirming Dev Renner's identity, which should have been reassuring, but not if Lena and Dev were confederates. Ellie's eyes went back and forth between Dev and Lena, looking for any sign of contact between them. She saw none.

Now it was Joel's turn to move in.

"How did you find us?" he asked, "And how do you know so much about us."

"I've admired your exploits from afar for a long time." replied Ishmael. "I was aware that you were responsible when all those people wound up in the wrong bodies years ago. As horrible as it seemed, I understood that you were trying to expose an experiment that had gone on far too long. Ends do sometimes justify the means." Ishmael scanned Joel's face and towering body with a look of recognition. He was familiar with Tobias Batie's body from its presence within Ganymede, first as the incarnation of Ethan and later as Connor Campbell.

Ellie and Joel exchanged looks of concern. The intruder's motives better be friendly because he seemed to know far more detail about them than she'd ever imagined. At best he could be an invaluable ally, at worst, a very dangerous adversary. It even occurred to her that with what he knew, he could even be a spy for Ganymede. If they let him stay, they'd need to watch him very closely. But what choice did they have? If they sent him away, he already knew too much and could lead the enemy right back to them. And without knowing whether or not he meant them harm, killing him wasn't an option.

For the second time in weeks, they would absorb a stranger into their midst and vet him as best they could. He held most of the cards for now, but they had the advantage of numbers. And Terra had been a skilled enough operative that if there were more to learn about Dev Renner, she would surely be able to discover it.

"You can stay," Ellie said at last, "but at least for now you're just a farm hand. Joel will show you to your cabin. And tomorrow you'll accompany Lara in the fields."

Lena smiled. She knew exactly how Mandala initiated newcomers. This city slicker would surely wind up his first day covered in horse shit.

The women watched Joel lead Dev from the cafe before anyone spoke. Ellie stared at Lara, trying to read what she was thinking. Lara was the first to break the silence.

"I know when someone's lying," Lara began, "and his story doesn't add up. There's obviously a lot more to it, but it will take some time to find out. Meanwhile, Joel and I will stick with him like glue. And we'd probably best keep Macklyn out of sight, at least for a while. He could even be a Ganymede spy."

"His story does check out," said Lena. "According to the UDB, he made a fortune trading in digital currencies. He was brilliant and ruthless at what he did. And he made dangerous enemies."

"So we should trust someone known to be devious?" said Ellie.

"And where's he been for the last five years?" added Lara. "Nobody vanishes into thin air on the UDB, even if he covered his financial tracks on the Dark Web." She paused a moment, lost in thought, the fingers of her right hand tapping on the table.

"There's something else," she said at last, both palms planted firmly in front of her. "Something about the way he moves is so familiar...It feels like I've known him before."

16

WHEN CORINNE returned from the hospital, she appeared the frailest Natasha had ever seen her. It was as though she'd aged ten years in just a few days. The skin of her hands appeared thin and fragile between the visible tendons on the surface of her hands, reminding Natasha of the webbed fingers of the other world's beings. And her hold on life was beginning to look as tenuous as theirs.

She was desperate to help, but Corinne was having none of it, at least so far as the prospect of joining their circulations to infuse Corinne with some fraction of Natasha's vitality. It seemed only reasonable since Natasha's body had drained Corinne's of its life force in the first place. But as much as she pleaded, Corinne held fast. Her mother's determination had always been unwavering once her mind was made up. Natasha would have to find another way.

She'd heard folklore as a child about dolphins having mysterious power over human illness. There were tales of them detecting diseases in some people long before they were found by conventional medicine. In the distant past, some people made pilgrimages to the sea to swim with dolphins in search of a cure, much as Catholics had sought cures by bathing in the waters of the spring at Lourdes. But such pilgrimages had ended after the changes in the climate had driven the aquatic mammals far out to sea.

Now Natasha had reconnected with these magnificent creatures. Perhaps she could use her newfound ability to commune with them to learn something of their healing powers. She was torn between seeking another encounter and staying close by her mother's side. She had no idea how long her mother had left.

Just as disturbing, the music was beginning to fade. She could still hear it faintly in her shadow consciousness, but it threatened to extinguish at any time. Natasha was becoming as terrified of losing contact with the other world as she was of losing Corinne. It was as if the preternatural hitchhiker in her consciousness was slipping toward oblivion along with its dying civilization.

Days turned into weeks. Corinne's illness confined her more or less to home despite her longing for the community and music of the Church. Then one Sunday, Natasha and Marcus carried her to the car and into the Church of the Double Helix. Upon entering the Church, Corinne's eyes lit up and the life returned to her face. The congregation welcomed her in as the resonant strains of the pipe organ rose toward their crescendo.

Natasha breathed deeply. Here was another place she felt at home and at peace. The holographic images of the double helix danced on either side of the dais as the minister made her entrance resplendent in sparkling robes. The minister raised her hands above her head and motioned the assemblage to be seated. As they settled in their places, the music from the organ came to a halt.

But the music never stopped for Natasha. Its melody rose in strength from the shadows, drowning out the words of the minister and beckoning Natasha away. She welcomed its return and surrendered, letting everyone and everything around her fade away.

She floated upright, naked in the watery world she'd also come to love. She was back in the open water outside the hives and the water was clear as far as the eye could see. The turquoise orb was clearly visible far above. The sea around her teemed with life. Another being floated to her side and touched fingers, much as it had during her first visit to their world. The hives were all on one level exactly as she'd first seen them.

What was happening? Had the music brought her back for another look at the beginning or was this a peek at an alternative future? She listened to her body, which felt comfortable and still. There were no longer pangs of starvation. To the contrary, she felt satiated and content as though she'd just consumed a bountiful feast. She looked at her companion, who also looked at peace. There were no signs of hunger or distress. And yet, something was off.

Natasha took in the details of the scene around her. To her right fifty meters or so away was a mass of indigo and green. As she glided toward it, what had looked like a solid wall resolved into a tangled mass of vines. She swam through a chink in the mat, emerging on the other side to what looked like fruit attached everywhere to branches projecting from the foliage. The fruit seemed to hang sideways, buoyed by the water, a parody of an earthly tree.

She reached out and plucked a piece from its branch. Round and deep purple, it fit into the palm of her hand, resembling a cross between an apple and a grape. She risked a bite, letting the juice flow across her tongue and spill from the corners of her mouth. The juice was luscious and sweet. It was how she imagined ambrosia might taste. She savored the flavor, indulging until the pleasure began to wane. When she was done, she felt no fuller than when she'd started to eat.

She moved about her watery garden, sampling a variety of its bounty, enjoying bursts of delight with each new item. By the end of her spree, however, she felt no more satisfied than when she'd begun. This was an Eden with endless opportunities for sensual gratification and no limits on what she could comfortably consume, but all the pleasures were fleeting. And once the novelty had worn off, there was no longer anticipation or joy.

She left the garden and cruised around the village of hives, her companion at her elbow. What else was different from her original visit to this paradise? All the bodies looked sleek and fit. There were no elderly...and no juveniles. Only young adults in the prime of life, mingling randomly, casually and fleetingly coupling, much as she'd seen images of earthly dolphins sexing in groups. Missing from these couplings was bonding, conception, procreation. This generation was forever for themselves. Endless indulgence awaited, but no anticipation of new life, new love. The circle of life was closed for eternity.

Her companion met her eyes, acknowledging her understanding of this place where nothing was wanting. It should have been paradise except for missing something essential to all sentient beings: longing. Without ever having to dream of things beyond reach, life was plundered of meaning and every moment became much like every other, an eternity of pleasure from which there was no escape.

The music rose and swelled. The hives disintegrated in front of her, replaced by straight rows of pews filled with people, listening to the final chords of the sacred music emerging from the great pipe organ at the front of the Church of the Double Helix.

The music was back. When the final strains of organ music had faded away and the congregation filed out of the church, the melody played on in Natasha's head. Her hitchhiker had stolen another ride with her from its world to hers, bridging the divide with its inscrutable chorus. Now, though, the music had changed. Behind the dominant melody was another, softer yet distinct warbling in a cadence that seemed to lament the futility of the world she'd just experienced.

That world was clearly further along the timeline of its universe than any of her previous visits, but how it came to be and what it meant eluded her. Had the music not returned or had it returned but not changed, she'd have guessed that it wasn't real, just a dream or her imagination. She reflected upon the multiverse. Some theorists from the early days of its conception believed that there were an infinite number of alternate realities branching into parallel universes from every moment in time. Perhaps she'd been misdirected to such an alternate future in a parallel world. That might explain the variation in the music. But why would she have been sent there and how did it fit into the narrative of the Creators?

She looked down at her mother sitting beside her, still frail, but blissful in this sacred place surrounded by friends, uncertain of what tomorrow might bring, but ready to accept whatever comes. Her precious mother, all the more precious because she could be lost in a heartbeat, clinging to her life, longing for another day.

17

ABRAHAM WATCHED from the beach as the drone returned from its mission. He'd watched remotely while it fired its missile into the midst of the school of sharks at a member its algorithm had detected as different from the others and had seen it strike and sink its target. But had it been Ishmael's vessel? He couldn't be sure. The traitor could be dead, or he could now be in the wind. Of all the people in his command, there couldn't have been a more dangerous defector. Ishmael had been his most brilliant disciple and knew everything about their technology.

Gabriel appeared from around the bend running along the beach at a frantic clip. When he'd finally reached Abraham's side and had caught his breath, his tone was urgent.

"We have a problem," he began, "a malfunction in the Brain."

"What's the problem?" asked Abraham. The Brain was the control center for every device on the island.

"It's the whole system. It's completely down. We can't control any of our electronic modules. All our functions are now on manual."

"What happened?"

"It looks like a bug...like the whole system's been sabotaged. But our firewall should have been impenetrable. It would have to have come from the inside. Where the hell is Ishmael? He needs to get to the bottom of this."

"I'm afraid Ishmael is already at the bottom of our troubles," said Abraham, shaking his head. "He's vanished.

And he's probably corrupted the programming before he left."

"Then that would explain our other problem," said Gabriel. "We've been getting garbled data from the Burning Bush. Now it's stopped communicating entirely with our MELD chips. It's like it's slowly self-destructing."

"Fucking Ishmael!" yelled Abraham, thrusting a fist in the air. "I hope to God he's dead."

Abraham's next challenge would be determining whether or not the drone strike had been successful in taking Ishmael out. As granular as the satellite images of the area were that were accessible on the UDB via his MELD chip, there was no way to visualize the depths clearly enough to identify a vessel on the bottom, particularly one disguised as a shark. He would have to have eyes directly on the site.

He summoned Esau and Rachel, two of his best trackers, and dispatched them in the hovercraft to the place where the strike had occurred. He programmed the drone to return to the same coordinates and launched it. Esau and Rachel followed.

When they arrived hours later at their destination, the drone hovered in place directly above the target area. They searched the ocean floor, moving in ever widening circles, but found nothing that stood out from the natural ecosystem. Even the carcass of the unfortunate shark that had drawn the fire had long since been consumed by the scavengers of the sea.

With the help of the drone, they surveyed the surrounding islands for signs of human activity and found the remnants of Ishmael's last campsite. When they searched the island by foot, they found his kayak hidden beneath a cover of palm fronds. He'd been there, they reported back to Abraham, but there was no clue how or where he headed next.

"What happens now?" thought Abraham. Ishmael had crippled Lazarus and he had the ability to inflict more damage, which he would surely do as soon as he had the chance. They would need to find him quickly and destroy him if they were to contain their losses. But someone would have to return to civilization to search for him, adding to the risk of the world discovering their presence.

Abraham summoned the boat back to Bethany Island. It returned empty, navigating on autopilot with Ishmael's kayak in tow. They would need it to resume fishing to nourish their people, another crucial function that would have to go on without Ishmael's expertise. Rachel and Esau were to remain behind and await further orders. Their new jumping off point would make it harder to trace them back to Lazarus.

Even with the power of their MELD chips and the worldwide satellite surveillance system, finding Ishmael would be like looking for a needle in a haystack. He could have wound up in Samoa or anywhere on the Pacific Coast from Japan to Australia. And it wasn't just location. They'd have to search recordings of each location over days. Unless he showed up in multiple images, locating him even by algorithm would be tedious. And Ishmael was Abraham's top operative. He would have been careful. He'd know how to hide.

"Eyes on the ground," thought Abraham. "In the end, the only way we'll find him." The closest destination would be Samoa, the logical first place to look.

"Samoa," he instructed his pair of operatives. They'd know what to do. Find discreet transportation on the Dark Web from their anonymous atoll in the Pacific. Pick up his trail. Find him and terminate him.

*****

Rachel found an outfit known to the undercover world that provided passenger drones and gave their coordinates. This flight would originate in Japan. Without a pilot, there would be one less witness to their identities. Hours later, the craft appeared overhead and landed in a clearing by the beach. They climbed aboard, setting the course for Samoa.

Rachel was silent throughout the nearly two-hour flight. If she'd had a choice about her partner in this mission, Esau would probably have been last. She'd never liked him when they'd worked together at Ganymede and liked him even less in their second lives. He'd always been crude and ruthless. And in his powerful new body, he became arrogant and impulsive, hard to trust in a life or death situation to have her back.

The mission itself was troubling enough. Her thoughts went back to Ganymede, where she and Ishmael, then Alec, had enjoyed as much of a friendship as their work in covert operations permitted, a friendship that stayed sufficiently low key to elude the notice of the Director. Despite their 32 year age difference and Alec's homely, scruffy appearance, she'd felt some attraction for him, charging their interactions with an undercurrent of flirtation. While her feelings were reciprocated, Alec respected the boundary of physical involvement out of respect both for the difference in their ages and the jeopardy that such an involvement could bring.

Her mind wandered to their early days on Bethany Island, where she and Ishmael suddenly found themselves contemporaries, inhabiting bodies both youthful and stunning. The nascent attraction between them in their previous incarnation blossomed into an overwhelming passion that neither could resist for long.

She'd initiated their first rendezvous on the beach after six weeks on the island, meeting his kayak at the end of his day's fishing, just after sunset, dressed in nothing but a thong bikini. He stepped onto the sand stinking of sweat and fish, at the same time embarrassed and overwhelmed with desire. His shyness, reminiscent of his self-consciousness in their previous life, just added fuel to her passion.

She dropped the bikini top, then the bottom and stripped off his clothes, taking him by the hand and leading him into the water. One plunge into the waves and his body was cleansed. They embraced, savoring a long, luxurious kiss that had waited years to happen. Then she wrapped her legs around his powerful hips. His hands gently cupped her buttocks as he plunged deep within her for the very first time. In fact, it was the first time for them both in their new bodies.

They'd risk meeting again only two more times during their two years on Bethany Island, the most recent only five weeks ago. It was too dangerous under Abraham's watchful eye to betray a connection that might run counter to his vision of the mission. But the rarity of their trysts only made them all the more delicious.

Now Ishmael was gone, and she'd been sent to kill him. She'd been loyal to the Director and to Abraham until now. Would she have the fortitude to adhere to the mission and follow orders to execute her lover? Perhaps Abraham had been not so oblivious to their liaison and had sent Esau with her to ensure that she followed through.

An island appeared in the distance, the largest they'd seen since arriving on Bethany Island two years earlier. As they got closer, she could see a necklace of emerald through the clear water surrounding the island, the living reef flourishing anew after near annihilation in the early part of the century. Samoa once again thrived as a tourist destination both from the West and from the East. The spectacular view broke her reverie and rescued her, at least for the moment, from her grim dilemma.

18

LARA KNOCKED loudly on the door to Dev Renner's cabin just before dawn the next day. The mist was rising from the ground and hung like a curtain just above the cabin's roof.

"Up and at 'em, cowboy," she called through the door. "Time to earn your way with an honest day's work." She heard footsteps on the other side of the door. It creaked open. There was Dev, no longer looking like a dude on vacation. He was dressed in the rumpled work clothes and shit kickers that Joel had left for him the night before.

"Ready." His smile lifted the corners of his moustache and was almost disarming.

"Come along, then," Lara said without smiling back and climbed aboard the cart. When he was aboard, they headed for the paddock.

The first task of the day was mending fences. Despite keeping up with this job almost daily, there were hundreds of feet of four board fence and there were always loose or rotting boards that needed fixing. Today, there were only three, but they were all sixteen footers. Two were on straightaways and one curved around a post at a corner and would need to be fastened with tension.

Lara watched Dev closely as he assisted her. She could see that he was strong, but not necessarily out of proportion to his size. He was thin, but powerfully built and his muscles rippled under the load. He looked like a man who took care of his body.

They replaced the two straight boards, then began working on the corner board, the second from the top and waist high. Dev held one end while Lara pounded the nails into the fencepost at the other. She watched as he brought his end toward the post around the corner. When the middle of the board made contact with the corner post, the board began to strain with the curvature. As the end pushed against Dev's midsection, his pace slowed and he appeared to strain, but managed to make contact with the fence post.

"Stop!" she shouted. "Just hold it there." She moved to the corner post with three long nails between her lips, then fastened the board in the middle with just a few blows to the head of each nail. Her speed was appropriate to her skill and experience and did not betray her own extraordinary strength. Then Dev nailed his end down, taking a few more strokes than she had to sink each nail.

When they were done, they both stepped back to admire their work. The board was straight and aligned perfectly with the ones directly above and below, standing out by virtue of the intense black color of fresh creosote in contrast to the faded black of the older boards. It would be months before the color faded and blended in, taking its place in the continuing life cycle of the fence.

Next Lara opened the gate to the paddock, led Dev inside and handed him a shovel. She gave him the same instructions she'd given Lena on her first day. Dev laid into the work without a grumble. The mist over the valley had finished burning off and the sun shone brightly, now halfway from the horizon to its apex. Dev worked steadily, but was barely breaking a sweat.

Lena was already starting her breakfast when Dev appeared in the doorway to the cafe. She beckoned him to join her, wrinkling her nose as he took his seat. He'd washed up, but still reeked of manure.

"I see you've been initiated," said Lena, smiling. "Been there. Far cry from writing stories...or trading currencies."

"Not so bad," said Dev. "A refreshing change from a sedentary life. Although, refreshing may not be quite the right word."

Lara sat down beside Lena and stared at Dev.

"You're a mess," she laughed. "Having fun, yet?"

"Actually, yeah. Change of pace from my usual routine. I think I like being close to the land."

"Then you've come to the right place," said Lara. "We've got plenty of dirt."

"How about you?" asked Dev. "How long have you been farming?"

"Long enough. It's home now. I belong here. Hard to imagine I've ever lived anywhere else."

"Where else have you lived?" asked Dev.

Lara stared at him. An innocent question?

"Doesn't matter," she said after a long pause. "I'm here now. That's all that counts."

After breakfast, Dev followed Lara outside, ready to go back to shoveling manure. She turned to face him.

"Good news, Dev," she said. "No more manure for today. We have roofs to repair. Hope you don't mind heights."

"Not at all. Lead the way."

The first repair was to one of the single-story structures adjoining the cafe. Two bundles of shingles sat against the base of the wall. Together they carried the extension ladder and propped it against the eaves. Lara ascended first and asked Dev to bring one of the packages of shingles up with him.

He slung the bundle over one shoulder and began climbing the ladder. Lara watched him closely. He moved steadily but seemed to struggle a bit to balance the load. When he reached the top, he slid the shingles onto the roof, then clambered off the ladder. Lara picked up a spade that was lying beside her and proffered the handle end to Dev, then pointed toward the crest of the roof where some of the shingles were broken or missing.

Dev pushed the edge of the spade under the leading edge of a row of shingles. They came loose and slid past him, tumbling to the ground. He repeated this action on another couple of rows. Then together they laid the new shingles in place and nailed them down.

There weren't many places left where asphalt shingles were still in use. Most structures now used roof coverings that contained integrated solar collectors. Renewable energy had dominated the civilized world for more than two decades and Mandala was no exception. But wind proved a more reliable choice in the Willamette Valley. Windmills dotted the landscape around Mandala's perimeter, more than meeting their energy requirements.

The next job would be more challenging, a barn roof two stories high. The repairs would also be more extensive, requiring five bundles of shingles. It would take at least an afternoon to complete. It again fell to Dev to carry the bundles up the ladder. He showed appropriate signs of strain for carrying a load to such a height. When he'd laid the last bundle on the roof, he paused to rest, but he was neither sweating nor breathless.

They worked side by side for the next couple of hours. Dev lost his footing once, but recovered. When they'd finished and were working their way back down the slope toward the ladder, Lara's foot slipped, and her body skidded toward the edge.

Dev reached out instinctively to grab Lara by the wrist and hand. She jerked her arm sharply downward. Dev tumbled past her over the edge, landing hard on the ground. When she looked down, he was lying motionless on his back. She scrambled down the ladder to his side.

He was still not moving, but his eyes were open and his breathing was regular. There was blood on the ground by his right elbow, but no signs of broken bones.

"Are you OK?" asked Lara. "I'm so sorry. I guess I panicked for a moment and was trying to break my fall."

"I'll be fine," answered Dev. "It's not your fault. Just got the wind knocked out of me."

"Your elbow…" Lara was looking at the large blood stain on his sleeve. "Let me look at it." She unbuttoned his sleeve at the wrist and slid it up over his elbow.

There was a two-inch gash just below the joint, but the bleeding had already stopped. Dev clapped a hand over the wound, but she'd already seen enough. Her instincts had been right when she'd decided to put him to the test. He wasn't an ordinary human. She knew the signs. He was like her.

The look in Dev's eyes told her he knew he'd been made. She held him by the wrists and was ready for a fight. But there was no fear in his eyes or hostility, only acceptance.

"Who the hell are you?" she demanded. "The Director sent you. Didn't he?"

"No. Nobody sent me. I came here on my own. And I'm on your side. Lazarus...Ganymede must be stopped before it's too late."

"Who are you?"

"Alec, Terra. It's me, Alec. I was once your friend, and if we're both to survive, you're going to have to trust me."

"Alec," Lara repeated, letting it sink in. Of all her former colleagues, he might well be the one she could trust. He was an honorable man and had once expressed doubts about the mission. While he'd been loyal to the Director, he had a sense of right and wrong and was one of the few people she could imagine refusing an order if it would bring harm to innocent people. She released his arms and sat beside him.

"What's Lazarus?" she asked next.

He told her the story of Ganymede's regrouping as Lazarus, eleven souls including the Director...now Abraham, patriarch of an island community preparing a powerful machine that would enable them to resurrect their project and eventually to dominate the world.

"They called me Ishmael," he continued, "and I was the architect of the Burning Bush, the machine that would aggregate the power of all our MELD chips to create the most powerful AI on the planet. I crippled it before I left. But they'll eventually rebuild it. And they'll come after us to make sure we don't attack it again."

"So what now?"

"We need to prepare. They'll look for us like I found you, searching satellite imagery and ground surveillance on the UDB. We'll need to throw them off. I might know a way."

19

IT WAS TIME for a strategy to keep Lazarus at bay and find a way to destroy them. For the moment, Mandala had the advantage. As far as they knew, Abraham had not yet discovered their location and had limited knowledge about the composition of their group. Ishmael knew the exact location of Bethany Island and the numbers and identities of the colleagues he'd left behind.

The first order of business was to slow down their pursuers. Ishmael had two tools he'd devised for evading visual searches on the UDB. Since he knew exactly what public places he'd passed through where he might have been caught on camera, it was a relatively simple matter to project negative images back to the same coordinates in place and time that would cancel the images on the record. The erasure would leave an anomaly in the record that could eventually be detected, but it would buy them some time.

Creating decoy images would be more complicated. Ishmael hacked holographic projection devices in Tokyo, San Francisco, and Denver that placed lifelike images of him in real time on the streets of those cities that would become part of the record of activity in those locations going forward. By staggering those images over several days, he simulated an alternative flight path that might send his pursuers on a wild goose chase. It would only be a matter of time before Abraham saw through this ruse, but it could buy them days or weeks.

Ishmael filled the others in on the remaining composition of Lazarus. There were ten left, including Abraham, all seasoned operatives who would provide formidable opposition. He could think of only one that could perhaps be turned. Her name was Rachel. They had a history together and had privately discussed the mission. While she was loyal to Abraham, the Director, she'd voiced some misgivings about his objectives and his methods. He'd sounded her out about participating in a mutiny, but she'd been steadfast in her loyalty.

They explored their options. They could launch a physical assault or cyber attack on Lazarus, or enlist the help of covert agencies operating within the government of the Commonwealth. Either approach would tip their hand about their existence and their location. And Abraham still had connections within the community of spy agencies, including moles within those agencies that would make any contact risky.

Another possible resource was Marcus Takana, the Minister of Discovery. Lara thought he could be trusted, and Lena was certain of both his integrity and his discretion. She'd be willing to be a go between if they wanted her to make contact and could do it discreetly without betraying Mandala's presence to the outside world. The scientific community over which Marcus presided operated largely off the radar of the intelligence agencies.

Contacting Marcus was important for another reason. Lazarus was intensely interested in both Lara's daughter Macklyn and Marcus's daughter Natasha because of their hybrid Ambrosia status. Marcus had to be warned about Natasha's jeopardy.

Any contact via the UDB, even with encryption, would run the risk of interception and expose their location. The information would best be delivered face to face. Lena was the logical choice. She was on a wagon the next morning to Cottage Grove, then a bus to Eugene. She rode the vacuum tube from Eugene to Portland and from there to Washington, DC. It took her more than a day to get from Mandala to Eugene, but just an hour from Portland to DC, nearly three thousand miles away. Her car delivered her to the Takana compound just after sunset, her second visit to their home.

She approached the gate on foot. In response to her presence, a holographic image of a pert young woman with a pixie haircut materialized just in front of the gate, greeting her with a welcoming smile.

"Lena Holbrook," said the woman. "To what do we owe this honor?" The nuance of the question and its intonation told Lena that Photina's machine learning had advanced since they last met. She'd become more and more sentient every year.

"I'm here to see Marcus and Corinne." Lena answered. "Please let me in. Privacy is paramount for what we have to discuss."

The gate swung open. An electric vehicle rolled up with the tangible version of Photina in the driver's seat. She invited Lena to sit beside her, then drove her to the front door.

Marcus met her at the door with a hug, which she found disquieting. In the past, it would have been Corinne greeting visitors first. Marcus saw the question in her eyes.

"Corinne's not been well," he said. "She's resting in bed, but will join us later. She'll be delighted to see you."

"What's the matter?" asked Lena, following him into the kitchen.

"I'll let Corinne tell you herself," replied Marcus. "It's her story to tell. But I gather this isn't just a social visit."

"Unfortunately, no." She paused, deciding where to start. "We need your help."

"We?"

"Lara...Terra, and Mandala," she continued. "They are all in danger and so are you and your family. Natasha is in danger."

"Natasha? Why?"

"Because of who she is...half mortal and half immortal. They want to study her biology, to find out what happens to the offspring of people who've had the Conversion."

"They?" Marcus was beginning to put together the pieces. "Ganymede?"

"Yes, Ganymede. You must have known they'd be back, given what they did. They've regrouped on a remote Pacific Island, eleven of them, now ten, and call themselves Lazarus. They all now have youthful bodies, bodies that have had the Conversion. And they want to know everything about how they work, including what happens to their offspring."

"Which is why they would be after Natasha," said Marcus.

"And Macklyn," added Lena.

"Macklyn?"

"Lara and Joel's...Terra and Connor Campbell's daughter. She's also a hybrid of Lara's immortal genes and Connor's normal ones."

"This is a lot to take in."

"Sadly, there's more. They sought to recreate their technology so they can resume their quest for world domination. And they've come up with a far more powerful version that they call the Burning Bush, a processor that aggregates the power of all their MELD chips as well as the worldwide network of MELD chips that they can access. When it's fully up and running, it will be virtually omnipotent."

"How do you know all this?" asked Marcus.

"From a defector named Ishmael, known to us as Dev, which was the name of his host. He escaped the island and found his way to Mandala to team up with them and Terra against Lazarus."

Marcus paced a few steps, deep in thought, then sighed deeply.

"Natasha's not here," he said.

"Where is she?" asked Lena.

"I wish I knew," he replied. "She's always been so independent and headstrong. She's been spending a lot of time by herself lately, working on some mystery. She hasn't told us much, just that she'll tell us all about it once she's solved the puzzle. She disappears sometimes for hours, sometimes for days at a time. And when she's around, she's been distracted, like she's in another world."

"Then how do we find her?"

"We can only wait for her to make contact. She's shunned her security detail. She routinely gives them the slip and keeps her location tracking turned off. The last time she left home, she wound up in Savannah. Came back muttering something about learning to feel distances. If she were anyone else but Natasha, we'd be worried about her sanity. But I'm sure she has a logical reason for her behavior."

Lena's eyes went to the kitchen doorway. Marcus followed her gaze. Corinne was standing at the threshold, leaning with one hand on the door frame, listening intently. She looked worried. How long had she been listening?

Lena was shocked at Corinne's appearance. This once robust and regal presence had aged at least a decade since they'd last met. She was gaunt and frail.

"Is Natasha in some sort of trouble?" asked Corinne. "I worry so when she goes off by herself."

"We're not sure," said Marcus, holding Corinne by the shoulders. "But we have powerful allies to help keep her safe. Do you have any idea where she might have gone this time?"

Corinne shook her head. "Who knows?" she said. "Off chasing ghosts. She left early this morning." She took a few steps, sat down next to Lena, and took her hand in both of hers.

"It's good to see you, Lena," she said with a twinkle in her eye, "even if you bring troubling news." She read the question in Lena's eyes.

"I seem to be dying," she continued, the smile never fading from her eyes. "It's quite a thing. Marcus gets experimented on and I wind up with the fatal side effects."

Lena listened intently, trying to understand.

"Bearing his child, our extraordinary child, seems to be more than my mortal body could stand. Her fevered metabolism must have sucked the life out of me. My immune system is shot, and I've been aging at least twice as fast as normal. I was lucky to have survived the pregnancy. Her body must have loaned me just enough energy for us both to survive."

"It's because of the Ambrosia Conversion," Marcus added. "When Natasha was conceived, she got half her genetic material from me and half from Corinne. Since I'd had the Conversion and Corinne had not, she was half immortal and half mortal. The immortal half of her development consumed an inordinate amount of energy and resources."

"Which is part of what Lazarus wants to learn," said Lena. "What happens when someone with the Conversion mates with an ordinary human being?"

"Then what happens now?" asked Corinne. "How do we protect our baby?"

"I don't know," said Marcus, shaking his head. "They have the advantage of sophisticated covert skills, which I don't have. If I reach out to the NSA or the CIA, we can't be sure that it won't leak back to Lazarus. They may even have spies in the President's inner circle. I'm afraid Terra's overestimated my power to help."

"Then all we can do is wait," concluded Corinne, "and have faith that a higher power is watching over her."

20

ABRAHAM SCANNED the UDB for Ishmael's locations over the time period since his disappearance by searching the record for matches with archival images of Dev Renner. Such searches had long made it difficult for fugitives to hide from the authorities or for estranged spouses to hide from the wrath of those they'd abandoned. They also made Witness Protection a procedural nightmare that gave many criminals second thoughts about turning state's evidence. Even plastic surgery was an ineffective disguise against the most sophisticated artificial intelligence.

He stumbled first upon the image that Ishmael had planted of himself in Tokyo, deploying Esau and Rachel there to find him. Then he discovered the sightings in the record in San Francisco and Denver, but something felt off. When his cyber experts examined the images from multiple angles, scanning backward and forward over time, they saw the moments the images popped into view and later out again, exposing the ruse.

Going back over the record, he looked for further anomalies, evidence of tampering with the record on the UDB. Ishmael was a master at such deception. With the help of his other agents and the combined resources of their MELD chips, they were able to search the Pacific Coast from Japan, down the coast of China to Australia and New Zealand.

Gabriel was the first to detect the ripple in the record from Port Douglas. They managed to amplify the image and separate it into its positive and negative components. When they subtracted the negative image, there was Ishmael, standing in a doorway, talking with another man. It was child's play then to identify the other man, the driver of the car that Ishmael had commandeered. Within hours, Esau and Rachel were in Port Douglas.

Rachel spotted him first, getting into his car. She grabbed the driver's door as it was closing.

"We need to talk," she said. "Get out of the car." By that time Esau was by her side. The man had little choice but to comply.

"You were here last Tuesday," she said, "a little after noon. We believe you met a stranger who may have asked you for a ride."

"That's right," said the man. "We met in front of the coffee shop over there."

"Where did you take him?" Esau demanded.

"To the Cairns airport," answered the man. By this time, he'd guessed that his answers could put his former passenger, who'd treated him generously, in mortal danger. He didn't volunteer details.

"Take us there," ordered Esau. "Get in." Esau took the shotgun seat and Rachel climbed in the back. This time there were no negotiations and no offer of payment.

The car drove to the main terminal and pulled up to the curb.

"Which airline?" demanded Esau.

When the man hesitated, Esau guessed that he'd been misled.

"Show me exactly where you dropped him off," he ordered. "It wasn't here, was it?" He showed a gun for the first time.

The man had no choice but to comply. Esau could have searched the car's computer, anyway, to determine the earlier destination. He pulled away from the curb, left the public part of the airport and swung around to the back road on the perimeter.

When they arrived by the side road at the gate that led to the hangar, they found the gate closed and locked. Esau shot the driver a look.

"Someone opened the gate when we got here," said the man. "They seemed to be expecting him. We drove right into the hangar."

Esau and Rachel got out of the car. He ordered the driver to get out, walked him to the edge of the woods, and executed him with a sharp twist of the head, while Rachel looked on in horror. He pulled the body into the woods, then programmed the car to drive a couple of miles down the road and veer into a ravine.

"That wasn't necessary," she said when he'd returned to her side. "He probably had no idea who he'd helped. He was just a bystander."

"Yes it was," replied Esau. "We can't have witnesses."

Within minutes, Esau was scaling the chain link fence, vaulting the barbed wire at the top and landed on the other side. His landing was as light and graceful as a gazelle. He motioned Rachel to follow suit and she was soon on the other side. They crept up to the hanger, found a side door ajar, and peered inside. The twin engine two-seater stood gleaming before them. The pilot was putting the finishing touches on its maintenance, readying it for its next journey.

Rachel looked on as Esau sprang from the doorway toward the pilot and held him at gunpoint. Her heart sank. She'd wished the hangar had been empty because she knew how this was likely to end.

"Where did you fly the man you met last Tuesday?" asked Esau. "Show me your flight plan."

They climbed into the cockpit together. The maps came up on the screen, along with the exact path the plane had followed to Eugene. An indicator on the screen showed that the plane was fully charged. Its range was sufficient to cross the Pacific. They climbed down from the plane and Esau commanded the pilot to open the hangar's bay. Once it was open, he marched him outside and out of sight. Rachel heard a stifled scream. Then Esau returned alone.

"There's only two seats," he said, looking her straight in the eye and shrugging. "No room for him."

This time, she said nothing at all. There would have been no point. She struggled to banish the chilling images of Esau's brutality and focus on the mission. They were preserving humanity, after all. What did two lives mean in comparison to saving billions? She tried not to think of what Esau was likely to do to Ishmael when they found him, or how painfully Ishmael might die. She knew that Esau bore personal malice toward Ishmael beyond the revenge that Abraham had sent him to exact.

Back in the days of Ganymede, Esau had been an operative for decades and had worked his way up through the ranks to become the Director's right hand man, groomed to be his successor. The Director had been ready to retire into his second life in a new body if he'd died under ordinary circumstances and to let Ganymede go on without him. But that wasn't meant to be.

Esau had still enjoyed Abraham's favor when they'd first assembled on Bethany Island until Ishmael conceived the Burning Bush. Ishmael's brilliant brainchild captivated Abraham's imagination and propelled him to the most trusted position by Abraham's side. Chasing him down on

Abraham's behalf to kill him therefore now felt particularly sweet.

They climbed into the cockpit, where Esau programmed the identical flight path that the plane had taken days before. Sitting shoulder to shoulder with Esau in the cockpit of the plane as it crossed the sea, her revulsion for him swelled. How cruel to team her up with a man she despised in pursuit of the one she loved. But they'd all been trained to kill, sometimes ruthlessly, in the service of their country. Country, after all, came first. And Abraham had instilled in them the idea that the mission went even beyond country to saving the world.

By the time they landed in Eugene, they'd finished tracking Ishmael all the way to Mandala. Once on the ground, they arranged for a pair of one man drones to take them on the last leg of their journey. As the aircraft landed with barely a whisper, Esau smiled. That night was a new moon. They would arrive in silence and total darkness at a remote corner of the compound.

To Esau, it was an unbelievable stroke of luck that Ishmael had wound up at one of their prime targets, the home of Terra and her daughter, one of the hybrid children from which they might learn the fate of their race. Abraham would be pleased, indeed, to eliminate his two most despised enemies and capture a prize, all in one fell swoop.

They were aloft just before midnight in a moonless sky, floating several hundred feet above the Willamette Valley, then swooping lower as they approached the walls of Mandala. They swooped in from the southwest, far from the gates to the compound and from the sentries on the walls by the entrance. They landed softly just inside and sent their craft unmanned back over the wall to lay hidden in the woods until needed for their escape.

Then they split up. Esau found a hiding place in one of the barns, while Rachel was deployed to explore the town.

She was relieved to be on her own at last after days as the captive audience of a monster. The streets were empty and the storefronts dark. There were a few scattered lights in the cottages on the back streets. She crept up to one and peered in the window.

Ellie sat alone inside, both hands extended from bent elbows, hands flat and fingers flying, jabbing the air as she stared intently at the space in front of her. Rachel tried to breach Ellie's virtual workstation, but it was impenetrable. This primitive looking farm was endowed with security that rivaled even the sophistication of Lazarus. Concentrating on the room's occupant, she missed the violet light blinking in a corner of the ceiling.

Then there was a hand on her shoulder and another covering her mouth. She moved to rise, but the force holding her down was a match even for her extraordinary strength.

"It has to be a SPUD," she thought, without considering the other possibility.

Ellie turned toward the disturbance at the window, walked over and opened it. She looked straight in the eyes of the kneeling woman, then at the man standing behind her, holding her down.

"Good work, Joel," Ellie said. "Bring her around to the cafe. I'll call the others."

Joel pulled Rachel to her feet, one hand still on her shoulder. She began to speak.

"Shh!" he commanded. "Not here. There will be plenty of time to talk soon. And I can't wait to hear what you'll have to say."

Once in the cafe, Ellie searched her, finding no weapon, then pointed to a chair. Ellie sat directly across from her. Rachel sat and regarded her captors, assessing her chances of escape. Ellie would be no threat, but Joel had already overpowered her once. She looked him up and down. Then a flash of recognition.

"Not a SPUD," she thought, remembering him from the last days of Ganymede when he was the captive. "Connor Campbell...an immortal like me." He'd changed his appearance, shorter hair, no beard, but it was unmistakably him. She turned toward the sound of a door opening. Lara walked in. Rachel took a sharp sudden breath.

"Terra," she thought, remembering her from their last encounter at Ganymede. Rachel still held an advantage since neither Terra nor Connor had ever seen her in her current incarnation. And Ishmael was nowhere to be seen.

"Where's Dev?" Ellie asked Lara.

"Finishing some repairs on the roof. He'll be along in a while."

Rachel recognized Ishmael's host's name. There would be no concealing her identity once he was present. She'd have to come clean.

"So tell me, Darlin'," said Ellie. "Just who the hell are you and what are you doing in our home?"

"My name is Rachel. And I've come looking for Ishmael, the man you call Dev."

"Why are you looking for him?"

"I've come to warn him," Rachel said, sliding into the groove of her story.

"About what?"

"About the others who are coming to kill him."

"And why would you warn him?" asked Ellie. "How do we know that you weren't sent to kill him?"

"I was, in fact, sent to kill him, but I couldn't," Rachel replied, "Because we...have a history together."

"Did you come alone?" asked Lara, watching her eyes closely.

"Yes," answered Rachel, controlling her breath and facial expression. She'd been trained, like Terra, not only to detect lies from micro-expressions and eye saccades, but also to suppress these signs during interrogation.

"How did you find us?"

"Abraham, our leader, tracked Ishmael on the UDB. I found the pilot who flew him here from Australia. The rest was easy."

"And you came alone?" Lara asked again.

"Yes, alone."

Ellie had been watching her closely while Lara questioned her and was the next to speak.

"How far along are you?" she asked.

"Huh?" replied Rachel. "What are you talking about?" She had no idea what Ellie meant.

"You're pregnant," said Ellie. "How many weeks?"

Rachel was dumbstruck. She looked at Ellie in confusion. Ellie laughed out loud.

"What's so funny?"

"You're a spy, trained to observe every detail, and you haven't even figured out you're pregnant. I knew it the first time I laid eyes on you. I can tell when a woman is pregnant in a heartbeat."

Rachel's hands instinctively went to her breasts. In the thrill of the chase, she'd barely noticed the tenderness in her nipples. Now she remembered the nausea she'd felt upon awakening the last few mornings that she'd attributed to the dread she'd felt in Esau's company. She recalled her last intimate meeting with Ishmael and did the math in her head. She was just short of six weeks pregnant with his child, the child of the man she was sent to kill. Tears were now streaming down her cheeks.

"This history you have with Ishmael," Ellie said, pointing to Rachel's belly. "Does it have anything to do with this?"

Rachel sobbed, too undone to speak, but her eyes told Ellie everything. Then Ishmael entered the cafe. As their eyes met, hers were full of turmoil, his filled with questions.

Ellie rose from the table and left the room, motioning Lara and Joel to follow. Rachel and Ishmael were alone, eyes still locked, on the cusp of choices that would seal their futures and perhaps the future of humanity.

21

ISHMAEL SMILED tenderly at the lover he'd thought he'd never see again.

"Then you decided to join me, after all." he said.

Rachel averted her eyes. He'd know in a heartbeat if she lied.

His smile dissolved. "You're not here to join me, are you?" he said. "You're here to kill me." His voice was filled with sadness.

She'd been ready for him to be angry. That she could have borne. But his disappointment stung. She could not push back against that.

"The mission," Ishmael said. "You've always believed in the mission, and in Abraham, even after he went off the rails. So are you still planning to kill me?"

"I was," she confessed, "but now something's changed." Her eyes followed her hands to her belly, where they rested. She looked him in the eye for the first time. Her eyes were wet with tears.

"You're pregnant?" he said. "How long have you known?"

"I didn't," she replied. "Ellie figured it out. I found out just before you came in."

"It's mine?"

"Of course it's yours. I haven't been with anyone else. I love you."

"And yet, you came to kill me."

"Yes. I was willing to sacrifice what I cherished most for the greater good."

"The greater good," he said. "You still believe that?"

"I do...at least I did. All of a sudden I have no idea what to believe." She held out her hands. He took them, drawing her to him.

The ice had melted between them. Ishmael took her in his arms. She nestled her head on his shoulder. But as happy as she was to be in his embrace, she couldn't bring herself to tell him that she wasn't alone. Abraham's influence was powerful and his reach long. In her decade and a half of service to Ganymede, she'd never considered betraying him.

Ishmael took her by the hand and led her to his cottage. When the door shut behind them, his hand lighted on her belly, where it lingered before sliding between her legs. Within minutes, their clothes were on the floor and she was straddling him.

For just this moment, there was no Lazarus, no Abraham, no mission, and no Esau. If only this could be all that mattered. If only they could be together forever, with no strings to the past and no consequences.

*****

As Ellie watched Macklyn turning cartwheels down the street from the cafe, an arm reached out from a doorway, grabbing her in mid-air and suddenly she was gone. Ellie lunged toward the last place she'd seen her granddaughter, but stopped short when she saw the gun at Macklyn's head.

Esau stood before her, still grasping the wriggling child.

"Bring me Ishmael," he demanded, "if you don't want the child to die."

Ishmael and Rachel had just returned from the cottage and dashed from the cafe together. Esau pointed the gun at Ishmael.

"Esau, wait!" Rachel implored.

The report of the gun filled the street. In its too silent aftermath, Ellie watched Rachel's body arc, as though in slow motion, in front of her lover, catching the bullet in mid chest, then fall with a sharp thud to the ground. Ishmael, bleeding from the right side of his rib cage fell on her, shielding her body from further injury.

Lara and Joel were in the street, guns drawn, but held their fire for fear of hitting Macklyn. Esau had turned and, still grasping the child, was sprinting toward the approaching drone, rope dangling close to the ground.

As Lara closed in on him, he managed to snatch the rope with his free hand. The drone lifted sharply, carrying him over the wall of the compound. He was soon out of sight.

Blood pooled around Ishmael and Rachel. When Ishmael finally rose to his knees, the wound in his chest had already stopped bleeding. Rachel lay motionless face down. Ishmael turned her onto her back. Blood still oozed from the gaping wound in her chest. Her eyes were wide open, staring lifeless at the sky. Even with her extraordinary body, there was nothing anyone could do to save her. From the anguish in Ishmael's eyes, Ellie knew that she was gone.

Lara and Joel were facing their own disaster. Their daughter was now in the hands of a ruthless killer. How had they let themselves be so blindsided? How could Rachel have withheld the knowledge that a second intruder was in the compound, determined to kill her lover and the father of her unborn child? She'd paid the ultimate price, sacrificing her own life and that of her child for his.

"Where will he take her?" asked Lara, once Ishmael had risen and turned his attention to the living.

"I don't know," said Ishmael. "Abraham will want to see her. They want to study her, find out what happens when someone with the Conversion mates with a mortal. But I'd guess he wouldn't go straight to Bethany Island since I know its location. Lazarus is probably picking up stakes as we speak."

"Where else, then?"

"Could be anywhere. Ganymede had safe houses all over the country. You'd know most of them. We also have stations offshore, some floating, and even one buried deep beneath the ocean floor. For now, they're in the wind."

"Not quite," said Lara. "Macklyn has a tracking device that I can follow."

"But Esau would be sure to detect it and remove it " said Ishmael.

"Not this one," said Lara. "It's integrated with every cell in her body and encrypted with her genetic code. It can only be detected and decrypted by someone who shares at least half her genetic endowment. That would be me."

"When we find them," said Ishmael, "Esau's mine. And he'll wish he were already dead. I swear I'll make him pay."

22

BY THE TIME CORINNE returned home from the hospital, Natasha was on her way back to Savannah for another rendezvous with the dolphin pod. While the answers to where we came from seemed to lie in the world of the Creators, she hoped that the wisdom of the cetaceans would provide answers to the pressing questions of the present.

She arrived in Savannah at nightfall and was up well before dawn, making her way back to the waterfront and the skiff that would take her out to sea. Eyes watched from the shadows as she emerged from her room and followed her on her quest. Even her enhanced sensory capabilities failed to detect the discreet presence of the skilled operative on her trail.

By the time Natasha was at the dock, light was starting to filter up around the edges of the horizon. The outlines of boats appeared scattered across the harbor. Then suddenly there was only darkness and a struggle for breath. The drawstring of the hood that now covered her head drew tight around her neck and an arm encircled her waist from behind.

"It's best not to struggle," whispered a female voice. "The hood will let you breathe as long as you don't suck it in."

Natasha wriggled in the grasp of her captor, but could not break free. While few humans were as strong as she was, this woman was more than her match. She gave up the struggle. The material that was obstructing her breath fell away from her mouth and nose. She could breathe again.

"I'm not here to harm you," said the voice. "As long as you cooperate, you'll eventually get to go home."

"Who are you?" asked Natasha. "And what do you want with me?"

"You can call me Delilah," said the woman, "and we just need to borrow you for a while. Now it's time for us to get moving."

Natasha heard a whirring sound above her head. The arm encircling her waist drew tighter and she felt her feet leave the ground. After ten or fifteen minutes, they touched down. The surface below their feet emitted a hollow, metallic sound. Then another clanking sound and she was directed to an opening, then down a steep stairway of six steps. Another sound just over her head signaled the closing of a hatch.

"Delilah?" she said. There was no response. She was alone.

Her hands were free. She felt for the drawstring around her neck and loosened the hood enough to slip it over her head. Now she could breathe more freely, but she was still in total darkness. She sat motionless on the floor, breathing slowly, and waited. The first ping came from her left, followed by others at intervals from all around her. Her sonar was mapping the contours of her prison. It was a spacious room, around twelve by sixteen feet and eight and a half feet high. There was no furniture at all. And no sign of the stairs by which she had descended into this space.

She sat and listened, probing her surroundings with all her available senses. Now she felt the gentle rocking of the floor beneath her. Whatever this room was, it seemed to be suspended in water. She placed both hands on one of the walls and felt the distant pings of sonar, emitted either by a creature or another vessel. If she were to find her way out of this compartment, she would still have to contend with an unknown expanse of water in order to reach freedom.

She listened for the music, but there was only silence. At least for now, it had left her, just when she felt she needed it most. There was nothing left to do. She closed her eyes and let slumber overtake her.

Natasha awoke to the sound of an impact from above, then muffled voices, and a whimper. She heard the sound of metal upon metal and a sliver of light opened above her head. When the hatch had slid all the way open, the stairs were lowered. Then a child, a girl of four or five, descended. The stairs were withdrawn. The hatch closed and she was again plunged into darkness. But she was no longer alone.

The child sniffled. "Where am I?" she asked.

"I'm sorry. I don't know," said Natasha. "I'm Natasha. What's your name?"

"Macklyn," answered the child. "I'm scared."

"How did you get here, Macklyn?"

"A bad man took me from my home on a flying machine. He shot a lady. He's a very bad man."

"Where is your home?" asked Natasha.

"Far away. He took me for a long ride inside a tube, then on another flying machine over lots of water to this place." She was crying again.

Natasha crawled to her and put her arms around her. The sobbing stopped, followed by gasping breaths, then slower ones. Macklyn snuggled into her embrace.

"You're not alone, Macklyn. I'm here to take care of you. How old are you?"

"Five." She held up both hands. Natasha put her hands around them and felt five fingers extended. She smiled.

"Who are your parents?" She asked next.

"Lara and Joel," said Macklyn. "They live on a farm. We have horses and a garden. My Gramma Ellie sometimes takes care of me. She's very old."

The crucial question began to emerge in Natasha's awareness: What did she and Macklyn have in common that they were brought here together? Her father was a powerful man, the Minister of Discovery. Her first thought had been that she was kidnapped for ransom or to get her father to do something that the kidnappers wanted. But Macklyn was abducted from a farm. Not a likely target for ransom or extortion.

Natasha was also aware that she possessed extraordinary abilities, powers that derived from her father's genes, which had been endowed with the Ambrosia Conversion. She was extremely strong and nearly invulnerable. She could be injured, but always healed way faster than any of her peers.

"Tell me Macklyn," she asked next. "Are you like other children?"

"Mostly yes," said Macklyn.

"Mostly? Are there ways that you're different?"

"I can jump over the fence around the corral. And I can do lots of cartwheels without stopping."

"Do you ever get hurt?" asked Natasha.

"Oh, yes. All the time. But it's OK."

"Why is it OK?"

"Because I get better real fast. My Gramma says it's magic."

"It is magic, Macklyn. I have it, too." There was now a special bond between them that was also the reason they'd both been abducted and brought to this place. She was now responsible for protecting them both. What did these people need from them? And how could she keep them from getting it?

There was one other clue. Delilah was no ordinary woman. An ordinary woman couldn't have overpowered Natasha and certainly not as easily as she did. Which meant that Delilah was either a SPUD, or she was like them, an extraordinary human being, one who had the benefit of the Ambrosia Conversion.

23

THE MUSIC had been gone for days, ever since Natasha's last ominous visit to the world of the Creators. Had she witnessed the last gasps of their civilization? Had they now left her forever?

Natasha's reverie was interrupted by a clanking of metal as the hatch above her head slid aside. She was blinded by the flood of sunlight streaming suddenly into the compartment. She instinctively shut her eyes tight and looked away from the opening, then let the light in bit by bit with a squinting gaze. A swarthy woman's face peered down at her from the opening.

"Time to go," the woman said.

"Where are we going?"

"You don't need to know. Now come up on deck, both of you."

Natasha went first, taking Macklyn by the hand and shielding her body with her own. Once on the surface, she could see that there were two captors, a man and a woman. The man was fair complexioned, with a face that might have been handsome had it not worn a permanent looking scowl. The exquisiteness of his underlying features only added to his intimidating presence.

They were standing on a platform about half the size of a football field, surrounded by open water. There was no land in sight. A pair of drones hovered just above their heads, dangling harnesses within arm's reach. Natasha heard the gentle whirring of their electric motors.

Delilah fixed one of the harnesses around her body, then grasped Macklyn by the waist. Esau put on the other harness and pulled Natasha close to him. As their bodies touched, her stomach turned. The girls were still holding hands as the drones lifted off.

The whirring of the motors increased in intensity and pitch, blending harmonically. Then the music of the drones subsided, replaced by the rising music in Natasha's head. She held tight to Macklyn's hand as they began to spin and the world around them faded away.

Then they were on the ground, the four of them now separate. No drones, no harnesses. Macklyn's little hand remained firmly in Natasha's grasp. Natasha gave it a squeeze and took off running. Macklyn took her cue, keeping pace. They had a head start on Delilah and Esau, who were still disoriented by the unexpected journey.

Natasha had no idea where she was. This world was not anything like any previous version of the world of the Creators. It was, in fact, more like her own world, peopled with human looking beings within a landscape of rectangular buildings that looked stacked, one on top of the other. The place was dense with standing people, so many that there was barely room to run while winding in and out among clusters of bodies.

As they wound their way through the throngs, she noticed that they all looked very similar to one another, all young adults, men and women all at the peak of physical fitness and beauty. Natasha and Macklyn stood out from this crowd as the only children. Even so, they attracted little attention from the teeming mass of humanity.

What was most chilling about this scene was in the faces of the people. They were alive, but expressionless. Their bodies were living, but their eyes looked dead like people who had long ago lost sight of any future worth living for as they milled endlessly in circles.

Through the milling crowd, Natasha heard footsteps approaching at a rapid clip. Esau and Delilah appeared, their heads bobbing among the heads of the crowd. The girls kept running and weaving, but their pursuers were gaining on them.

She heard a gunshot. One of the milling throng came suddenly to life and leaped in front of her, catching the round in his shoulder. He fell momentarily, but was soon up and blending back into the crowd. More shots. More people throwing themselves into harm's way, all but one recovering instantly from their wounds.

Natasha turned to see a body just behind her, a woman felled by a bullet to the forehead. She lay still in the road, face up, eyes wide open beneath the bullet hole, a smile frozen on her dead face. Their interference was saving the girls' lives, but the grim truth dawning in Natasha's awareness was that these were not acts of heroism. They were desperate bids to die. What kind of world was this? Was it a glimpse of our future?

Suddenly her hand was empty. When she turned back from the body in the street, Macklyn was gone, carried away by the tide of bodies. Then Esau and Delilah were almost upon her.

She took off through the crowd. Her pursuers split up, Esau following her and Delilah now in search of Macklyn. Natasha ducked into an alley and caught a brief glimpse of Macklyn dashing past the other end with Delilah in close pursuit. By the time she reached the opening, they were both out of sight. Esau rounded a corner and was again on her tail.

Shots were fired. More bodies fell around her. Esau was now firing randomly in her direction to clear the path between them. He was not shooting to kill her, she concluded. For whatever reason, he needed her alive.

As fast as she was, the wall of bodies impeded her progress. Esau was closing in, still firing his weapon. A body dropped in front of her. She stumbled and fell. Before she could get up, his foot was on her shoulder, pressing her down. Then she heard the music rising.

"Macklyn!" she screamed. But Macklyn was nowhere in sight as this strange world faded from view.

Natasha heard the whirring of an electric motor. She and Esau dangled from the rising drone as it swung away from the platform over open water. She seized the opportunity of Esau's surprise at their sudden return to the present to release his grasp and dropped into the water. She sunk thirty feet before the buoyancy of the water arrested her fall, hung motionlessly for seconds, then rose toward the surface, at first slowly, then accelerating as the force of the water lifted her body.

She broke through the surface just in time to see the drone descend toward the surface of the water and drop Esau twenty feet away. Natasha stripped down to her underwear to reduce the water's drag on her body and swam as fast as she could. But even fully clothed, Esau's powerful body kept pace just a few body lengths behind her.

A ping stung her thigh, then another and another until a solid rain of pings descended all over her body, signaling the approach of the pod. The swarm of dolphins soon filled the space between her and Esau, pushing him back. He broke the surface as the drone descended toward him, grabbing the harness. The drone rose sharply, pulling him free of the water.

Natasha came to the surface for air in time to see a second aircraft approach from the distance, closing fast upon Esau. Shots were fired as she resubmerged, taking her place among her aquatic escort. She could no longer see what was unfolding above the surface. And she had no idea what was happening to Macklyn in the other world.

24

LARA AND ISHMAEL followed Macklyn's signal all the way to the east coast before it went out to sea. Then it vanished abruptly.

"That's not possible," said Lara. "Nothing can interfere with this signal as long as Macklyn is alive." A wave of horror washed over her at the possibility that her daughter could already be dead.

"Don't jump the gun," said Ishmael. "There has to be another explanation."

They summoned a pair of drones and set out over open water toward the last location from which the signal had transmitted before it died. They scanned the area until they spotted the platform. Its surface was flat and bare. There was no sign of life.

After alighting on the platform, they explored its surface until they found the edges of the hatch. There was no handle or any sign of how to open it. It reminded her of Petra's kitchen when she'd first explored her house in Petra's body.

"Allow me," said Ishmael, pressing the toe of his right foot against one edge of the hatch. It gave way to the pressure and the opposite edge popped open. Lara had expected a biometric lock or some other more clandestine solution. This platform was low tech.

Lara pulled the hatch the rest of the way open. A folding ladder was attached to the underside. They descended into the unlighted space below and found it empty. She felt her heart skip a beat and a sensation of something round in the back of her throat. Anxiety had been an unfamiliar emotion during her lifetime as a covert operative. She'd never feared for her life. But her daughter's life...that was something else altogether.

They ascended the stairs to the surface of the platform. Lara sat at its edge, staring out at the endless expanse of ocean. Macklyn could be anywhere out there. Or worse, her body could be lying somewhere under the sea, lifeless and scavenged by predators.

Suddenly out of nowhere there was the sound of a motor. A drone came into view. From the distance, two people appeared suspended beneath it. Then one of the figures dropped straight down and disappeared into the sea. While the first figure was still submerged, the drone swooped down toward the surface, depositing its other passenger, a burly looking man, into the water, then rose again to a holding pattern above the action.

Ishmael was now by Lara's side, watching the drama unfold. It appeared to be a chase. The second, larger person swam with powerful strokes and was gaining on its smaller prey, perhaps a woman or a child.

"Esau!" said Ishmael. "That has to be him."

"But that's not Macklyn," said Lara. "Who else could it be?"

Just as Esau was closing in on his target, a huge commotion erupted just under the water's surface between the two swimmers. When the disturbance ended, the fugitive was nowhere to be seen. The drone swooped down within Esau's reach and lifted him out of the water high above the surface, headed straight for the platform. But when he spotted the two people on the station, he reversed course.

Ishmael was aloft in moments and the chase was on. As Lara watched, the adversaries sped toward the horizon until they disappeared from view.

Her attention was then drawn back to the water where a pod of dolphins breached in unison just off the edge of the platform. When they'd plunged back into the depths, a young woman floated face down, her feet rhythmically pounding the water, propelling her toward Lara. Lara reached down, grabbed her by the wrists, and hauled her sharply onto the platform.

"Thank you," said the girl when she'd caught her breath. Her wet hair hung in strings around her face as she looked straight in the eyes of the stranger who'd rescued her.

Lara gasped.

"Natasha," she exclaimed. "Natasha Takana." Even after six years, her face was unmistakable.

"How do you know who I am?" Natasha asked, alarmed at the possibility that this was another of her pursuers.

"I knew your father from before you were born. I'm called Lara now, but he knew me as Terra."

Natasha knew the story of her father's bizarre contract to sell his body. She knew that it had been the origin of his obtaining the Ambrosia Conversion, which was the reason behind her own extraordinary powers. And she'd heard about the mysterious Terra, who'd been an agent of a shadowy clandestine operation designed to people the world with immortal beings in their control. She knew also that Terra had died while saving her father's life. That Terra had returned to life in another body was a wrinkle in the story of which she'd been unaware until now.

"What are you doing here?" asked Natasha.

"I'm looking for my daughter. Her name is Macklyn. She's five years old."

"Macklyn is your daughter?"

"Yes. then you've seen her? Where is she?"

"I found her…and now I've lost her," Natasha said.

"Lost her? Where?"

"That's hard to say. I think it was the future." She told Lara about how the music had drawn her into the world of the Creators and had apparently flung her and Macklyn, along with their captors into a world of perpetually young beings.

"I tried to protect her, but we got separated. When I was brought back here, she was left behind, along with Delilah."

"Delilah?"

"She's the one who took me. Amazingly strong. I think she's like us...like me...and Macklyn."

"I think you're right." said Lara. "She and Esau are both agents of Lazarus, which is made up of resurrected operatives of the organization for which I once worked." She paused. "So how does this work? How do we get Macklyn back?"

Natasha shook her head slowly. "I'm not sure we can," she said. "It's not like I've been in control of where the music takes me, or even when it appears. If I try to go back, I could wind up somewhere entirely different."

"What if there was a connection between us and the other side?" asked Lara. "Macklyn and I are connected with a special homing device. It got me this far in finding her. Then the signal disappeared when you crossed over. Maybe it could bring us both to where she is."

"I guess there's nothing to lose in trying."

The two women sat side by side on the platform, legs crossed in front of them, arms interlocked.

"Just close your eyes and breathe," Natasha said. They let their eyelids close almost all the way, concentrating on the rhythm of their breath.

Natasha heard the first strains of the music. Then Lara heard it, too, as it rose in volume, enveloping them both in its vibrations. Along with the music, Lara felt the distant signal of the homing signal connecting her with Macklyn.

"She's alive," Lara thought with relief. "Hold tight, Sweetie. I'm coming."

The world dissolved. When it again took shape, they were standing in the street amidst the milling throngs. But the ground beneath their feet was no longer stable. It was rumbling. Shallow waves of energy rolled beneath their feet.

"This way," said Lara, picking up the distant homing signal from Macklyn's body. They threaded their way through the crowd. It was almost impossible to get their bearings, so similar did their surroundings look in every direction. Lara thought she saw the tail of Macklyn's shirt flash from among a sea of knees.

The rumbling increased in amplitude. It was getting harder and harder to keep their balance as they ran. Then Lara noticed that the crowd was moving slower and slower until it stopped. Lara and Natasha stopped, too.

The people, standing in place, looked to the sky and raised their arms in unison. Then they all dropped to their knees in prayer.

Above the bowed heads, only Macklyn and Delilah were now visible among the crowd and still moving. Lara and Natasha gave chase. Delilah grabbed Macklyn by the wrist and ran. They turned a corner. By the time Lara rounded the corner, they were nowhere in sight. But all of a sudden, she saw familiar landmarks that had once surrounded the entrance to Ganymede's headquarters. Above the rumbling of the street, she picked up Macklyn's homing signal.

Within minutes, they were through a gate and in the secret tunnel. The signal's intensity mounted. When they emerged into a well-lit space, Delilah was there, still holding Macklyn by the wrist. Lara scooped her daughter in her arms. Delilah put up no resistance.

In the middle of the room sat a man, his back to them, laboring intently at a huge machine that glowed and pulsed in synchrony with the rumbling waves in the street. Sturdy muscles rippled across his back and broad shoulders. His head turned in profile. He had youthful features and smooth skin, but something in his eyes betrayed a tortured, ageless soul.

"Hello, Terra," the man said. "I'm glad you've come." The cadence of his speech was familiar, even though its timber was not. What she saw in his eyes astonished her.

"You!" she said. "How is this even possible?"

"My name is Abraham, now," the man said. "At least that's what it's been for nearly two centuries. I was the leader of Lazarus. We continued the mission, and as you can see, we succeeded. You've seen the world we created, a world of exceptional beings."

"Exceptional? How? Their minds are all blank."

"Quite the contrary," said Abraham. "Their minds are flooded with data. They all know everything there is to know. And their knowledge increases from moment to moment by orders of magnitude. Mankind has always believed that knowledge is power. I've given them what they thirsted for most. And before you stands my greatest creation, the Burning Bush."

"The machine you designed to harness the collective knowledge of all mankind."

"Not exactly," said Abraham. "That was its original purpose. But like everything else, it's evolved beyond what we intended." Now his voice had a rueful tone that was totally out of character for the Director she remembered.

"You must understand by now, Terra, that we were wrong."

"Wrong? About what?"

"About everything. About the mission. About what was good for the world. About power and what people wanted. We made a terrible mess of everything. Now it's up to me to fix it."

"Fix it? How?"

"With the Burning Bush. It was designed to link together the collective knowledge of the populace. But as I said, it's evolved to do much more. Now it can harness the collective will of the people and do its bidding. My role is to keep it running long enough to execute that will."

"What can they all want so badly?" asked Lara.

Natasha knew. She'd seen it in the streets during her first visit to this place. People putting themselves in harm's way on the remote chance that they might die.

"Relief," said Abraham. "All they want now is to shuffle off this mortal coil and have peace."

The machine glowed brightly. The rumbling grew louder.

"Leave now!" commanded Abraham. "You don't belong in this world and this time. This is not your fate."

The door to the room swung open. Natasha and Lara, still holding Macklyn, ran through it. Delilah turned to follow.

"Not you, Delilah," said Abraham, looking at her with both sadness and affection. "Your fate is with me. It was always meant to be. If I'd only realized that in the first place, none of this would ever have happened. How glorious our lives together could have been."

He held his hand out toward her. She took it in hers as the door swung shut.

Where were they supposed to go? Where would they find the portal, if it existed at all, back to their own time? They ran back in the direction from which they'd come. The streets were now rolling with greater force. Behind them, they could see the pavement crumbling and the buildings starting to collapse. The people were still on their knees, looking to the heavens and praying, they knew not to what.

Amidst the din of the rumbling, the music began to rise. Lara and Natasha both heard it and ran toward its origin. As they got closer and closer, the world behind them disintegrated. Then there was a flash, followed by a void that seemed to last for eons. And they were back home, in their own time, floating on a platform on the sea.

25

ISHMAEL HAD all he could do to keep Esau's drone in sight. The two drones and their human cargo were so perfectly matched that it seemed impossible to close the distance between them. When Esau fired his weapon, Ishmael lost more ground swerving to avoid the shot. How could he tilt the balance of the chase?

In a moment of desperation and resolve, he fired one round at Esau, then flung his weapon behind him into the sea. Between the drone's reaction to the force of his throw and the diminished weight of its load, he accelerated just enough to gain on his adversary. Esau fired again but the shot went wide. The intensity of the chase interfered with his aim. As Ishmael closed in, Esau flung his weapon at him in a last-ditch effort to break free. Ishmael easily dodged the missile. Then they collided.

Metal ground on metal as the rotors engaged, then broke off. The drones spun apart, then reengaged, fracturing another pair of rotors. The drones stalled in unison and plunged with their human cargo into the sea.

Ishmael hit the water feet first, plunging straight down into the depths. He saw Esau strike the water moments later, just out of his reach. Ishmael's powerful legs kicked to slow his fall, then propelled him toward his adversary. He caught Esau dead in the face with the top of his head. Blood swirled in tendrils from Esau's nose, staining the water around him.

Esau recovered from the blow and the mighty warriors locked arms, spinning together as they rose toward the water's surface, swirls of red still streaming from Esau's nostrils. Ishmael was the first to spot the torpedo like object streaking straight at them. Sunlight reflected off the razor-sharp teeth of the Mako shark as it closed in. Both men released their hold and raced away from the ghastly predator.

Ishmael was just one stroke ahead, but it was enough. He heard the churning behind him, turning just in time to see Esau's flesh shredded in the powerful jaws of the killing machine. Then he broke the surface for a gulp of air and swam with every ounce of remaining strength while the creature devoured its meal. Even with his superhuman body, he would be no match for this demon of the sea.

Within minutes, the shark had devoured enough of its prey to take interest in the fleeing man. As it barreled toward him, there was nowhere to hide. He was still too far from land to escape. His lungs were bursting. He would either die by drowning or be eaten. The latter, while terrifying, would be swifter. He burst one last time through the surface for a gulp of air.

The roar of a drone swooping close to the water filled his ears. A rope skimmed the surface, brushing past his face. He swiped at it with his right arm, caught it, and reached with the other arm to grab hold of the rope just above his right hand. The drone pulled straight up, ripping him from the water, the shark breaking the surface just beneath him, snapping at empty air, then crashing back into the sea.

Ishmael held tight as the aircraft banked and headed to its destination, the floating platform from which the chase had originated. When he finally looked up, Lara waved to him from the pilot's seat, a cheerful grin lighting up her face.

When they reached the platform, Lara made a slow pass that brought Ishmael close enough to drop onto its surface, then banked again and came back for a landing. Natasha and Macklyn sat together, watching the last of Lara's aerial maneuvers. Ishmael was relieved to see that the girls were safe, but wondered what had become of Delilah. Despite her adversarial role in their recent conflict, she'd long been a respected colleague in their previous life, and he'd borne no malice toward her. He'd once hoped that Abraham's obvious affection for her would eventually entice him away from his consumption with the mission.

"Delilah didn't come back," said Lara once she'd joined him, anticipating his question.

"Didn't come back? Then where is she?"

"She's stuck in the future," said Lara, "or at least whatever version of the future we just visited. And to the best of my knowledge, she perished there...along with the Director."

Lara filled Ishmael in, as best she could, on the strange journey she'd made with Natasha to rescue Macklyn from Delilah. She described the world of lost immortals that had been the unintended consequence of Abraham's misguided mission. Then she showed him a virtual replay of her final interactions with Abraham in which he affirmed his intention to put himself and all the others out of their misery forever.

"We have to stop them," she said at the end of her story. "At least, we have to try."

"But first we have to find them," said Ishmael.

"Yes," said Lara. "But I have an idea exactly where they would be."

26

PRECIOUS TIME had been lost to Natasha's encounter with Delilah and Esau, time that was critical to any chance of saving her mother's life. By the time she got back home from this latest journey, Corinne's health had deteriorated further and her hold on life had become even more tenuous.

As Natasha searched for answers to her mother's illness, the thought flashed through her mind that there might be an alternative reality in which Corinne was healthy. If only she could wriggle through the wormhole that connected that reality to this one. But that was wishful thinking. And if there were such a reality, would the music exist within it? If she had to choose, would she trade all of what she'd learned of the other world and the abilities with which she'd returned for her mother's life? Not a fair question. Even thinking about it felt like a dagger piercing her heart.

If she were bound to this reality, perhaps the juxtaposition of her otherworldly and worldly perils was meant to be. Maybe she could use the one to solve the other. Natasha recalled the stories of people having healing encounters with dolphins. In her own contact with them, she'd experienced a profound connection. They'd watched over her body while her consciousness was traveling between dimensions. But there was also a sense that they knew what she was feeling, perhaps even sharing her emotional experience empathically. And at the end of her first visit with them, she'd felt serene.

She laid out her proposal to her parents. They'd travel together back to her rendezvous point with the pod of dolphins off the Georgia coast, making the pilgrimage to seek healing for Corinne. It might be crazy and would certainly be risky for Corinne to make the journey in her precarious health, but it might also be her only chance to live.

Corinne's eyes lit up as Natasha spoke of communing with dolphins. She'd always imagined these magnificent creatures to be our brethren. When Natasha was just a toddler, she'd told her stories of human encounters with dolphins that envisioned the latter as possessing superior intelligence and wisdom. Corinne thrilled at the possibility of seeing them in the wild, a marvelous final scene as her life drew to its close. It hardly mattered to her whether or not it might save her life.

It took a couple of days to prepare Corinne for the journey. If the dolphins were to have the best chance to assess her biological functions, she might have to be in the water, no small feat for someone already struggling for breath. Natasha and Marcus assembled a stable flotation device that would allow Corinne to lie face down in the water. Once they got to Savannah, they would procure an oxygen tank to attach to another float alongside Corinne's to assist her breathing. Natasha would be right beside her.

The morning of their outing was overcast. Natasha was disappointed that her mother wouldn't get to see the glorious sunrise that had greeted her on her first excursion. They considered waiting for a day with better weather, but Corinne seemed strong and determined. They decided not to risk losing this window of opportunity. And the clouds would protect them from the sun's rays, which were far more hazardous to someone in Corinne's condition than rain.

Their boat was more substantial than the skiff Natasha had used when she was alone. It would get them to their destination faster and provided Corinne shelter from the elements. Natasha navigated to the shoal where she'd had her first encounter with the dolphins and dropped anchor. That time she'd been naked when she entered the water. With her father present, she stripped down to a tiny bikini and still felt embarrassed, but she needed as much of the surface of her skin exposed as possible to beam her sonar to the surrounding waters.

"Wait here," she told Corinne, and slipped into the water. As she glided downward into the silent depths, the music began to rise. Her heart began to pound, the rhythm beating in her ears in competition with the music. She'd always surrendered to the music, but now too much was at stake. She couldn't leave and abandon Corinne. She looked at her hands to stay focused on the present. The panic subsided. The pounding in her chest and ears eased and along with it, the music waned.

As the sounds in her head faded away, they were replaced by a swelling barrage of pings, rising in pitch and accompanied by a pleasurable tingling all over her body. Then she was at the center of a whirlpool swirling around her. They'd come. The moment of truth was near.

Natasha rose to the surface and signaled Marcus to lower Corinne into the water. She supported her from below to bring her gently to the water's surface. The oxygen tank on its float was already waiting alongside the boat. Natasha swung it into place beside Corinne, extended the tubing, and fitted the mouthpiece inside her lips to seal out the water. Corinne took a few deep breaths and signaled that she was at ease. Natasha slipped beside her, took her hand and waited.

The pings had receded while Natasha and Corinne had disturbed the water's surface. They were now barely audible. Natasha and Corinne floated and waited. They'd found her in the depths with her whole body exposed to the water. Could they still sense her presence on the surface?

With Corinne's hand still in hers, she shifted her body to a vertical position and floated just beneath the surface. Her skin began to tingle with increasing intensity. She could hear the pings, rising in pitch and volume. As the pod circled, the pings were replaced by new sounds: runs of clicks punctuated by whistles, varying from short and shrill to long and resonant. There were a dozen or more creatures, now slowly circling, showing interest in the human lying prone on the water's surface.

The dolphins brushed by Corinne, barely touching her as Natasha floated just beneath. They clicked as they approached and whistled as they withdrew. When they were circling again, the clicks and whistles formed a continuous interchange among them. They were vocalizing one at a time...having a conversation. What was most remarkable was that Natasha seemed to understand what they were saying.

"This one is special," they seemed to be saying, "She has given much, and her time is short." Natasha listened as the clicks and whistles mingled melodically, resembling the music that played ever so softly in her head. Their lyric soothed her.

"Embrace death," the song went on. "It is the sweetener of life." Then they were gone.

Natasha floated back to the surface alongside Corinne. She could see her mother's chest expand and contract in a slow, easy rhythm. Her body was otherwise quiet, peaceful. She signaled her father that it was time. He brought the boat around and they lifted Corinne out of the water. Natasha removed the mouthpiece and gazed into her mother's eyes. Her expression was blissful.

27

WHEN LARA AND MACKLYN got back to the mainland, they were met by Joel. Macklyn ran into his arms. He held her snugly to his chest, swaying back and forth in joy and relief. His tears glistened in her hair.

"It's good to have you back," he said to Lara. "For a while, I had no idea where you were."

"I'm happy to see you, too," she said, "but it's not over yet. There's still something I have to do. I have to find Abraham...the Director."

"I searched all over the Pacific," said Joel. "There was no trace of them."

"They're not in the Pacific," she said. "I figured out where they wound up. They're practically under our noses."

"Then where?"

"Back where they started from. In Ganymede's headquarters. Right in DC."

"How would you know that?"

"Because that's exactly where we found them in the future. So they must have returned there at some point. And why not now? It's been over five years since they staged their deaths. The facility has been shuttered, but all their technology was left intact. It would be the easiest way to retool the mission. And nobody would expect them back."

"So you plan to just waltz back into the belly of the beast? How will you get in and what in the world will you do when you get there?"

"That's exactly what I plan to do. Dev...Ishmael will come with me. We'll offer a truce so we can meet with Abraham."

"And then?"

"We'll talk him into abandoning the mission and destroying his creation, the Burning Bush." Her hands were held palms up in front of her, attesting to the simplicity of her plan. She was matter-of-fact, confident, as if she somehow possessed the key to her enemy's heart.

'Why can't we just let this go?" entreated Joel. "I almost lost you just now. I can't risk losing you again. Macklyn can't risk losing you."

"There's a lot more riding on this than us," said Lara. "Perhaps the fate of humanity. The greater good. I don't plan to die. But if I do, I know I can count on you to take good care of Macklyn, to raise her well."

Joel and Macklyn were on the next tube transport back to Oregon. Lara and Ishmael boarded a capsule to DC. When they arrived, they set off on foot toward the heart of the Capitol. They both knew their destination. They were back on familiar ground.

The entrance to the tunnel was now overgrown with shrubbery, no longer visible or accessible to vehicles. They wriggled through the overgrowth and descended the tunnel. On the wall to the right of the door glowed a pad in pulsating hues of reds and violets. Ishmael glanced at Lara. His new body lacked the biometric properties needed for entry, but Lara still possessed the hallmarks she'd fashioned for her incarnation in Petra's body that recreated her identity as Terra.

She held her right hand in front of the pad. The pulsing of the colors changed in tempo and the colors changed to blues and greens. Then she looked directly into the center of the pad. It went dark. She heard the creaking of ancient gears, then a sharp snap. The door slid ajar.

Ishmael slid the door the rest of the way open and they crossed the threshold. They were met by Gabriel, who was stunned to see these two familiar, but unwelcome visitors. He drew his weapon. Lara and Ishmael's hands remained by their sides. They offered no resistance.

"What are you doing here?" asked Gabriel.

"We've come to talk with Abraham," said Lara.

"Abraham won't be happy to see either of you," said Gabriel. "You've both betrayed him. And you know well that he's not a forgiving man."

"He'll see us," said Lara, "and he'll listen to what we have to say. We bring information that is crucial to the mission."

"Where's Esau?" asked Gabriel, menacing them with his weapon.

"He's dead," said Ishmael. "Eaten by a shark. I watched him die."

"And Delilah?"

"Gone," said Lara.

"Dead, too?" asked Gabriel.

"Maybe."

"Maybe? What do you mean?"

"It's complicated," said Lara, "a very long story that you're not likely to believe. Take us to Abraham and I'll tell you both at once."

Gabriel marched the captives across the chamber to a familiar door, then knocked.

"Enter," said a voice from within.

The door opened. Abraham sat with his back to the intruders, still focused on the machine before him that seemed to crackle with life. His sinewy arms and shoulders looked just like the man she'd left two centuries in the future. He turned to confront them. Abraham hadn't changed in 200 years, but there was no resemblance to the Director, the ancient personage she'd only seen backlit and shrouded in mist.

He peered at her with clear blue eyes, the color of which seemed bottomless, then glanced at Ishmael and back again.

"Terra!" he thundered. "The last time you were here, you destroyed us all. What makes you think you could walk back into my sanctum and live?"

"Hear me out," said Lara, "and if you still want to kill us when I'm done, then go ahead."

"And why would I let you live?"

"Delilah," said Lara. "This is about the mission, but it's also about what's happened to Delilah."

"What did you do to her?" he growled.

"Not me," said Lara. "It's what you did to her. You're responsible for her fate. And if she has any chance of surviving, only you can save her."

Now she had his attention. He fell silent for the first time and bid her with his bottomless eyes to tell her story.

She recounted the tale of her visit to the other world, seemingly the future, and the empty existence she discovered within a world full of immortals who longed only for oblivion. When she got to her encounter with his future self, his pupils dilated so wide that they nearly extinguished the blue of his irises.

"Why should I believe such a preposterous tale?" he bellowed.

"Wait," said Lara, "and I'll show you."

The space between them filled with an almost identical, smaller version of the room they occupied. Abraham and Lara were both there. So were Natasha, Macklyn, and Delilah. Abraham gasped at the vision of Delilah, reaching his hand out to touch her. But his hand passed right through her image. Then he saw himself talking. He leaned in to make out the words.

He heard rumbling in the background, saw the Burning Bush glowing and pulsing, and heard himself speak.

"You must leave now," commanded the virtual Abraham, "You don't belong in this world or this time. This is not your fate."

He watched Natasha, Lara, and Macklyn moved toward the entrance with Delilah close behind. Whatever was going to happen, she'd escape, too. She'd be saved.

Then his alter ego spoke again.

"Not you, Delilah," it said. "Your fate is with me. It was always meant to be."

Delilah hesitated, then stopped and turned. He saw his future self reach out.

"No!" shouted Abraham. "Save yourself!"

The rumbling grew louder. Natasha, Lara, and Macklyn were out of sight. The ceiling began to crumble over the images of himself and Delilah, burying them both. Then the image dissolved.

Abraham buried his face in his hands.

"So this is where the mission ends?" he asked. "This is the future I've created?" Any inclination he may have had to doubt her account was extinguished by the power and fidelity of the virtual scene, his own words, and the connection between him and Delilah that had been known only to him.

"Perhaps," said Lara. "Perhaps not. There may be something we can do to change it."

Abraham understood. His passion for the mission hung in the balance. If there was any chance of saving the love of his life, the mission and its instrument would have to be abandoned.

"Ishmael, my son," he said, "Forgive me. You were once my most trusted lieutenant. Now I need your help again. You were the architect of the Burning Bush. Only you know how to destroy it so that I can never bring it back to life."

Ishmael nodded. He took his place in Abraham's seat before the great machine that glowed and crackled with power. His hands and fingers flew in the air at blurring speed for minutes. The crackling grew louder. Then flames burst from the base of the machine, enveloping it.

"We must leave right now," said Lara to Ishmael. "If we succeeded, the future we visited will never happen. And we may not remember that future or what just transpired in this room. If Abraham never saw the images we showed him, he'll see us only as enemies who wrecked the Burning Bush." She began running for the entrance. "Come!"

Ishmael followed. As they emerged through the entry door into the tunnel and looked back, the fire had extinguished, and the machine had gone completely dark. Abraham stood glaring at them, looking bewildered. In the shadows beside him stood Delilah.

28

IT WASN'T THE ANSWER Natasha was seeking from their visit with the dolphin pod. She'd hoped to find a way to save her mother's life. Instead, they'd indicated that death was inevitable and had encouraged her to accept Corinne's fate. Natasha wondered whether she'd really heard the dolphins talking, whether the message came perhaps from the part of her that was still joined with the world of the Creators, or whether it simply gave voice to her own intuitive wisdom.

But as disappointed as Natasha felt, she'd never seen her mother more at peace. If she couldn't save Corinne's life, bringing her comfort as she came closer to its end provided some compensation. Corinne had always been a model of living life to its fullest. Now she'd blaze the trail to a fitting death.

As the boat sped back to shore, the rising music nearly drowned out the sound of the engine. It seemed now to be coming from the direction of the open water behind them. Once Corinne was safely back on land, the pull of the music became irresistible and Natasha set off again to sea by herself. The volume of the music swelled as she approached the place where they'd met with the dolphin pod. She dropped anchor, stripped to her skin, and plunged into the water.

As her skin tingled from the signals of the approaching pod, the music enveloped her and swept her away. She felt her body undulating as she propelled herself through the water toward a column of light in the distance. Her broad tail swept up and down as flippers kept her on a steady path forward. From the pings striking her broadside, she felt the presence of others keeping pace on either side of her and made out the outlines of creatures much like the dolphins in the world she'd just left. She was now one of them.

Her companions pulled slightly ahead and she followed their lead. The column glowed brighter, fully exposed to the surrounding waters, no longer encased within a network of hives. The light pulsed in an intricate pattern that seemed random at first. As she attended to the sequence, however, she noticed it repeating at long, regular intervals. She was witnessing a machine pacing the heartbeat of a world...a world devoid of humanoid life.

Much like the Eden like environment she'd last visited, the waters were clear and teeming with life. In the absence of the humanoid civilization's toxic effect on the environment, this world had restored itself, allowing most species to survive and thrive. But nature seemed to know better than to allow the human population to rejuvenate. All that was left was the machine they'd left behind, a machine that derived energy from the sun without sucking the life out of all that surrounded it, a machine that droned on endlessly without any further guidance from the life forms that had created it. But what now was its purpose? And how did it relate to the strange version of this world's future she'd last visited?

As Natasha attended to the repeating pattern of pulsating light, she became aware of a sequence of vibrations painting her body with strokes that felt synchronized with the pulsing of the light. The pattern was familiar, melodic. She recognized it as the music, now perceived tactilely by the exquisitely tuned sensors of her cetacean body. The music she'd regarded as an essential aspect of the Creators was now embodied within the energy of the machine. It was as though they were one and the same.

The column of light began to fade. The tactile pattern on her body now blended seamlessly with the music as sound returned to her world. Her body rotated slowly on the surface of the water as the dolphins bore her afloat in her own body. She could feel water swirling between her legs and in the space between her arms and body. She opened her mouth and inhaled deeply as she was welcomed back to this world with a cacophony of clicks and whistles.

The night air felt cold as she scrambled back over the transom into the boat. The evaporating water was drawing heat from her body belying the balminess of the weather. As she sped toward shore and her body dried rapidly in the rush of air around her, she was soon warm again. She reveled in the sense of vitality that accompanied these fluctuations in sensation and comfort. Being alive meant living in the constant flow of change around her. That idea lingered, poking at her consciousness until sleep took her, exhausted, from the world.

29

BY THE TIME Lara and Ishmael emerged through the shrubbery at the entrance to the tunnel, their memory of the world they'd just visited was still intact, but felt more like a scene from a movie than a place they'd actually visited. After Delilah's reappearance by Abraham's side, they felt confident that they'd succeeded in altering the timeline of this universe.

The image of Abraham and Delilah standing side by side brought painfully home to Ishmael that his love, Rachel, was lost forever.

Together they boarded the vacuum tube transport to Oregon. Lara was going home, but Ishmael was returning to Mandala to fulfill a sacred trust.

After Esau murdered Rachel, her body was placed in a biodegradable body bag, which the people of Mandala used to bury their dead. A transparent window left the face of the deceased visible. Once buried, the bag eventually decomposed along with the body, becoming one with the earth...dust to dust. This was in keeping with the community's dedication to preserving the environment. At Ishmael's request, however, Rachel's body bag was vacuum sealed and kept chilled until he could come back for her. It was now time for the last leg of their journey.

"Where will you go now?" Lara asked Ishmael as he gently placed the body of his love on board the helicopter.

"Bethany Island," said Ishmael. "Where Lazarus began. There are still things I must do to make sure that it never rises again."

"It was good to meet again," said Lara. "I wish you well. And if you ever get a craving to shovel manure, you're always welcome at Mandala." She grinned and held out her hand. He took it in both of his, held it for several moments, and said goodbye.

Ishmael caught a flight from Eugene to Samoa. From there, he took a hovercraft to Bethany Island, arriving just before sunrise. He cradled Rachel, still in the bag, in his arms, carried her ashore, and laid her on the sand. Then he sat beside her and watched the sun rise together one last time.

"I'm sorry," he said aloud. "If I hadn't left, you might still be alive."

For a fleeting moment, he realized that this was not only Rachel's second death, but also the second death of whomever this body once belonged to. Perhaps long forgotten, that person also deserved a respectful sendoff.

Once the sun cleared the horizon, Ishmael carried Rachel to the shade of a cluster of palm trees at the edge of the beach and covered her with fronds. Then he made his way to the village.

As expected, it was completely abandoned. The remaining members of Lazarus had all accompanied Abraham back to Ganymede's headquarters. The cottages were empty. Most of the digital gear had been dismantled and was gone. All that was left was the Burning Bush, it's hardware too massive to move, even in pieces, over the vast expanse of water between Bethany Island and the mainland. While Ishmael had crippled it before he left, Abraham had managed to restore much of its function before fleeing the island. This behemoth remained the last chance for Abraham to change his mind and resurrect the mission.

Ishmael returned to the hovercraft to retrieve the explosives he'd brought with him. Crippling the Burning

Bush's software wasn't enough. It would have to be completely demolished to eliminate its threat. He planted the charges around the entire perimeter of the machine, attached the remote trigger, and headed back for the beach.

He found his kayak where the last fisherman had left it in a thicket not far from Rachel's body. He pulled it waist deep in the water, moving it across the shoreline, and beached it close to the cluster of palms. Then he cradled her body in his arms one last time and placed her in the kayak.

She belonged in this place. He'd given much thought about where he might bury her before settling on his plan. They had consummated their love in the waters off the island. That would be her final resting place.

Ishmael paddled the kayak just beyond the reef that surrounded Bethany Island to his favorite fishing grounds. He opened the bag and slid it off her body, which, between the vacuum packing and the Conversion, was still almost lifelike. He looked one last time at her face, kissed her on the forehead, and lifted her over the transom into the water. Her body floated briefly on the surface before the sea claimed her forever.

Then he sent the signal to detonate the explosive charge. A massive fireball erupted from the middle of the island, accompanied by a thunderous roar, a military salute to a fallen soldier.

30

IMAGES FROM ANOTHER WORLD encroached upon Natasha's slumber. At the center of her dreams was the pulsating column of light. Musical notes swirled up the column, spilling out the top in all directions, scattering like popcorn. As the notes tumbled and fell, they sprouted gangly limbs, turning them into silhouettes of the people of that world before dissolving to shadows in the waters.

"The people are in the machine," was her thought upon awakening. "What could that mean?" She was lying in the bottom of the boat, looking up at a cloudless sky. The sun had already climbed well past the horizon, telling her it was midmorning. Her parents would already be back home.

She closed her eyes. Visions of the otherworldly Eden flooded her mind...the too perfect world. That was it!

The world of the future was so flawless because it wasn't real. It was a virtual world, digitally crafted in the dying days of their civilization to host the consciousness of the people. The machine was left as the curator of this world, a benign custodian without the power or insight to invest it with randomness and suffering, critical attributes of reality and crucial elements of meaningful life. All that was left was an eternity of hedonistic pleasure and satiety.

"If they were trapped forever in the machine," Natasha considered next, "then how have they been able to influence life in our world and to communicate with me through the music?"

Those would be questions for another day. Natasha's most immediate concern was her mother. The outcome of their pilgrimage was not salvation, but rather confirmation that Corinne was destined to die. How long she had was uncertain, but every moment apart was time lost with her. It was time to go home.

Natasha was by Corinne's side again well before nightfall. The excursion had taken its toll. Corinne's breathing was irregular, pausing altogether from time to time, but she remained conscious. The food that Marcus had brought her hours before remained untouched by the bedside. A faint smile played on her lips. She did not appear to be in pain.

Natasha realized that Corinne, who prior to the pilgrimage had fought for every breath of life, had surrendered to dying. As much as she valued life and her relationships with Marcus and Natasha, she'd never seen death as an enemy to fear and now appeared almost to welcome it. The lesson of the dolphins was one of tranquility. Corinne's eyes told Natasha not to be afraid.

Natasha took Corinne's hand in hers and sat quietly by her side. Her mother's hand felt tiny and frail. An hour passed, then two. She felt a momentary squeeze. Then the hand in hers began to vibrate, gently at first, then with greater and greater intensity as energy flowed from Corinne's body to hers. As the vibrations filled her being, the music filled her head. She braced for the voyage to the other world. So little time left. Couldn't they wait just a little longer?

Then she noticed her mother's lips moving. The music subsided. She leaned in to make out the words. The voice began as a whisper, then grew in strength and clarity. It was a strange voice, not Corinne's, and in a strange language with a rhythm and melody much like the music. But as the words took form, she could understand their meaning. And the hand in hers felt warm and full.

"I am Rimwe," the voice began. "I am the culmination of the civilization that you have visited and watched perish across the divide between your world and mine. Our race perished because we became greedy for life, prolonging it and growing in numbers until we exhausted our resources. We sought refuge in the machine so that our world could reclaim itself."

Natasha had been right about the virtual world that contained the consciousnesses of the lost people. They had found a version of immortality, but the eternity they sought proved to be more hell than heaven.

"We became trapped in an endless loop in our virtual world," the voice continued. "until we discovered that we could join our minds with others, blending identities to create new entities. We'd found a way to reproduce, but instead of multiplying our numbers, we became fewer with each generation. Parents blended to become their children. And as the generations progressed, we became strong enough and knowing enough to modify the program from within, finally freeing ourselves from the confines of the machine."

"I am the final generation, the merging of innumerable individual lives from the beginning of time. I am noone and everyone. I am pure energy and boundless knowledge."

Corinne's grip on Natasha's hand suddenly tightened and Natasha felt a thrill throughout her body. She inhaled deeply. The air rushing into her lungs and the oxygen flowing through her body were intoxicating. The scent of jasmine floated through an open window in Corinne's bedroom and her ears filled with the chirping of birds. The softness of Corinne's hand in hers was especially sweet. As she released the air from her lungs and it passed across her vocal cords, the strains of the music poured forth and filled the room for what seemed like eons.

When her breath was spent and the music stopped, Corinne's lips again began to move.

"The multiverse is my realm. I have missed only one thing: being alive and substantial, touching and being touched, yearning, exulting, grieving, and especially dying.

My connection with your world enables me to taste life as I flow through the people and creatures that populate it and as your spirits join with me in precious death."

Corinne's lips stopped moving. She took a long luxurious breath. Her hand fell limp in Natasha's. And she was still. Natasha felt tears streaming down her cheeks and tasted their salt on her lips. Anguish filled her heart, accompanied by an exquisite awareness of her own vitality and the place that grief had in sustaining it.

Her world fell silent. The music had left her, at least for the moment. Now that the story of the Creator had been told, she had no idea whether she would ever hear the music again. But she knew that if she did, she would hear Corinne's song too.

Epilogue

LARA WATCHED as the massive gates of Mandala opened to its latest visitors. Secrecy was no longer as crucial since Lazarus had been neutralized as a threat. Strangers showed up with increasing frequency to learn about their lifestyle, a model for sustainable living. But these two women weren't strangers.

"Lena, Natasha, it's so good to see you again," said Lara. It had been nearly a year since she'd seen either of them. Natasha had asked permission to visit and had invited Lena to join her. There was something she wanted to share with them all.

They met back at the cafe that evening. Lara, Joel and Ellie were there along with several of their closest friends.

"After my mother died," began Natasha, "the music came for me one last time and carried me back to the future. But this wasn't the future world we visited. It was an alternative future, a parallel world that evolved from the changes that Lara and Ishmael brought about after we returned to our own time."

"How was this world different?" asked Lara.

"Let me show you what I saw," said Natasha.

Lara and Joel moved all the tables to the edge of the room, leaving a large open space in the middle. Then they dimmed the lights and Natasha began the virtual show.

In the middle of the room materialized a miniaturized animated tableau of a village. People were in the streets, greeting one another with smiling faces. There were children playing at their parents' feet and people of all ages. The elderly inhabitants moved more slowly than their younger counterparts, but looked healthy and fit. The community appeared to be thriving.

A large screen in the middle of a park displayed a video of a stately elderly man. It was a memorial tribute on the hundredth anniversary of his death. Natasha explained that the man in the video was her father, Marcus Takana, who'd become one of the most beloved Presidents in the history of the United Commonwealth of North America. His presidency had heralded an unprecedented era of world peace that had been sustained for more than a hundred years.

Then an image of an elderly woman appeared on the screen.

"That's me," said Natasha. "I taught the lessons I learned from the Creators from another dimension that helped us lead the world to peace and sustainability. They are honoring my memory. I'd been dead for nearly half a century before this scene took place."

"I don't understand," said Ellie. "You carry the Conversion. You weren't supposed to age or die."

"Wait and it will become clear," Natasha said as the scene unfolded.

Their attention then became fixed on a figure at the edge of the park walking toward a gazebo in the middle. As the person came more clearly into view, it moved slowly, but resolutely, ascending the stairs to the stand amidst cheers and applause. When she turned around, the people in the room gasped in unison. She looked almost exactly like Ellie, complete with deep lines in her aging face and a smile that lit up the whole space around her.

Then another woman ascended the stand, the present-day Natasha visiting this future world.

"Hello, Natasha," said the older woman. "It's so nice to see you again after all these years."

"That's Macklyn," explained Natasha to the people in the room. "She's played a crucial role in history. She's the one who solved the problem of aging."

"The problem of aging?" asked Joel. "I thought the Ambrosia Conversion had already provided a way to stop aging."

"Not to stop it," said Natasha. "To get it started again. As you can see, people in the future are growing old. Even Macklyn and I eventually aged. Macklyn somehow understood from a very early age that mortality was what gave meaning to life. She'd had a vision of what life might come to be in a world of immortals and dedicated her life to preventing it. She told me we'd become close friends and that she'd been with me when I died."

The virtual tableau began to shimmer, then gradually dissolved. The room was silent except for the gentle sobs of its occupants.

Somewhere else, far, far away, Abraham and Delilah danced.

About the Author

Rick Moskovitz is a Harvard educated psychiatrist who taught psychotherapy and spent nearly four decades listening to his patients tell their stories. After leaving practice, he in turn became a storyteller, writing science fiction that explores the psychological consequences of living in a world of expanding possibilities, including even the prospect of evading death. His characters deal with enduring moral and emotional struggles against a backdrop of a near future world that is still dealing with environmental crises as it navigates the intersection of human and artificial intelligence.

www.ingramcontent.com/pod-product-compliance
Lightning Source LLC
Chambersburg PA
CBHW070923130626
46555CB00001B/261